Stranger Than Fiction

Stranger Than Fiction

DYNESTY

THE BEGINNING

Baby Jada is what they called me.

Even at 14, I was still compared to Jada Pinkett. My mom insisted on naming me Nichole even though my father said hell no. I was small, or what they would call petite. My complexion was lighter than Jada Pinkett's, though I was short with a cute little shape. I was a dancer, so my stomach was flat, my butt was nice, and I never really had any breasts. I always had pretty curly, thin hair that was sandy brown in color. My hair rested on my shoulders in the front and on the top half of my back. I have no idea where my hair came from because my parents had hair that was totally opposite of mine.

I'm assuming that I inherited my attitude, smart mouth, and demeanor from my parents. At 14, cursing was nothing new and my attitude wasn't new either. I gained street smarts once I started to really get out in the world and begin to learn myself. So, there wasn't any challenge for me to think on my feet or figure things out. I like to think that I can talk my way out of anything. As for school, it was a no-brainer. It came to me easily. I even picked up natural skills from my dad -- like building things from scratch with my hands and fixing things.

Life is what appeared to be normal. I had what I thought was the American dream. We had a nice sized three-story house, two cars, a tan picket fence, and a dog named Frisco. My family was perfect, too.

My mom's name was Denise. Man, oh man... my mom handled her business, and was a fire cracker when lit. She also can be as sweet is gold. She could be considered a very, very smart woman. My mom worked for the government since she was 19 years old and went nowhere but up ever since. She was a red bone – so light, in fact, that you can seen the veins in her face. My mom was petite as well, which is where I got my frame from. The difference between us was that she had what people would consider a nice set of breast but no ass at all.

My dad Westley was a tall, chocolate man. In fact, he was a purple-and-hard-to-find-in-the-dark kind of black. He's easily considered an alcoholic and a hell-raiser but hands down he was funny as shyt. At times he could be mean -- really mean -- but I guess if you knew him then you'd know he didn't mean much harm. My dad and I had so much fun together, too. He used to ask me if I wanted to ride to the store with him and we would end up in a whole different state. Maine, Philly, Chicago, Canada you name it we went. But what was crazy was that it was never planned. I loved my dad with every ounce in me.

Wannell is my oldest brother. He was the cool kid... the popular ladies' man. Everybody knew Wannell. All the ladies wanted Wannell. He was never really home when I was growing up, and once he graduated from high school he was off to the Navy. 17 years older than me. He was tall and slim, brown skinned with short hair, cute with a baby face and he was always fly. I adored him.

Graham and Brittany were both my younger siblings. This made me the second oldest, Graham the third child, and Brittany the baby. What was so crazy was that these two look liked twins and they were ten months apart. Their close bond enhanced their twin-like appearance. Brittany? She was my heart though -- my ride or die. Just like a sister is supposed to be.

Then there was my extended family which consisted of my grandma, aunt, and two cousins. Nell was the boy cousin who was closer to me than my biological brothers were. I used to call him Phats because during the time he was thick. He was also the typical light skin nigga. We just had a bond the really couldn't be fucked with. His mom was a beauty. Aunt Nette was maybe 5'7 and brown-skinned with a pretty smile. She had clear skin with a nice build and a little weight to her.

In 2003, my aunt found love. In fact, I could say she found the love of her life. His name was James. James was tall and had a really dark-skinned complexion. He looked identical to that 90s singer Brian McKnight. They had been together for a while and things appeared to be going well. The next thing I knew, my aunt was engaged and was getting married. For the first time in my life, I was asked to be in a wedding. Yea, that's right. Me. Nichole.

I accepted and held down the position on her special day. May 25, 2003 was the day of the wedding because it was also my aunt's birthday. I can only imagine what could have been going through her mind on that day.

After the excitement was over, life quickly went back to normal. Or at least, I thought it would.

My mom met this guy at her job. They were dealing with each other for a while, apparently. I didn't start to notice the affair until shyt got weird. Phone calls were made to our house, house visits were made. He just started popping up in our home life out of what seemed like the blue. And it all happened while my dad was away on business.

See, my dad wore many hats. He was a man of many talents. He could build a house and damn near fix anything. In fact, he's nothing short of a modern day super hero. In his efforts to keep saving our perfect home, he began trying to get his CDL. He made big bucks driving those big ass trucks on the highway back in the day. Of course, times were different because the law didn't require you to have one. But things change.

One of the days my dad was gone, he called the house from out of town to check on us. I answered, "Hello?"

"Hey baby girl, how are you? Where is everyone?"

"Hey daddy, I'm good. Brittany and Graham is outside in the yard with the dog, and mommy made a run. How are you what you doing? When you coming home?"

He sighed. "I'm doing ok just a little tired of driving. I have a few things on my mind. I'm coming home soon as the training is over, not sure of the exact date though. But hey let me ask you question baby girl."

"What? What I do?"

"Has your mom had another guy at the house? Or any company for that matter?"

Now, you can only imagine how uncomfortable I felt. The kind of pressure I endured at that moment. The things I thought were crazy and that I was tripping about were surfacing… and what was even more possible was that maybe I was being grown. Everything made sense now. Things were starting to add up. The even bigger question was why in the hell was he asking a 14-year-old about her own mom? What did he know? Or, for that matter, what did he think he know? Would I say something and fuck up my family? My American dream? My perfect life? Those were the million-dollar questions.

I hesitated, then replied, "Um nah not that I know of or at least I didn't see anyone. Why do you ask?"

"Well, have any men been making phone calls to the house?"

"No one but grandma. Daddy why are you asking? Is something wrong? Do you need me to tell her something or ask her something?"

"No, you don't open your mouth. If she asks you if I called tell her yea and let that be. That's all you do you understand me?" He paused and spoke gently, but sternly. "Listen baby, all this is probably too much and maybe I shouldn't be telling you this, but before I went away on training for my CDL a letter was addressed to me from someone at your mother's job. The letter had everything but a name. Whoever wrote the letter wanted me to know that she worked with your mom. The letter said basically that your mother had been having an ongoing affair with a man from her job. They go on lunch dates every day. They have been on a few trips together. The letter also read that this guy has been in my home and in our cars. So, Nichole it's a lot maybe too much for you to follow but under no circumstances are you to repeat what I told you understood?"

"I understand. I'll talk to you daddy. I love you."

"I love you too. Be good. See you when I get home, baby."

Damn... so this is what the hell goes on when people get married?! I literally didn't want to believe anything I just heard. The sound of his voice was heartbreaking. He sounded defeated. I was actually surprised he even told me because he always told me I better stay in a child's place.

3 Weeks Later

I was upstairs in my room, dancing to music videos when I heard the door slam downstairs. I knew it was my dad, so I flew with a quickness to greet him at the door. Before I could get there, all hell had already broken loose.

There was yelling.

There was screaming.

There was name calling.

On my left, spit was flying out of my dad's mouth with all sorts of horrible names to follow. As I looked to the right, my mom was yelling with tears streaming down her face banging on the counter. The next thing you know, my mother said, "Fuck you Westley, I'm leaving you! We are done! I can't do this... us... you... anymore! I'm taking my kids and I'll be back for our things. You can keep this precious house and all your bullshyt cause I'm out! You're a fuckin alcoholic, get you some fuckin help!"

My dad responded, "Fuck you Neise stupid cheating bitch! Do what the fuck you have to do. I'm going to drink till I die believe that!"

My mother got us a bag, made her a bag, and hauled me, Graham, and Brittany away -- just like that. My oldest Brother was in the United States Navy. He had been gone for a while and had no clue what was going on back at home (or at least what he used to call home).

This particular night we left home, but this wasn't like other times. This was different. We didn't run to grandma's house or get a hotel; we slept in a random parking lot near Paradise and Parkside. My mother ignored each and every phone call that came in from my dad. Let's just say that he was the type of guy that acted an ass and then tried to apologize later. It was safe to say that my mother wasn't rocking this time -- she didn't answer one phone call at all. She was completely done.

A month later, we were in our new place off of Minnesota Avenue.

* * *

By now it was the summer time, we were all settled in our spacious apartment. My mom signed me, my little brother, and my sister up for summer camp and she also obligated me to be responsible for them too, making sure they got from Point A to Point B without any issues. All of us would be going to camp at Fort Dupont Skating rink. Normally twice out of the week the camp was required to go on outings or field trips. In the meantime, until camp started, I went to my aunt's house. Occasionally, I visited either my grandmother or my aunt's house because they both were very close to where we had just recently moved to. My grandma's and I relationship was simple; we were very close. Non-stop laughs were all that occurred whenever I would come around. At one point my aunt and grandma were living together but once my aunt met her new flame, she moved out and made a new life of her own with her soon to be husband. She was never too far away if my grandmother needed her.

My aunt's and I relationship was cool, too. I kept her laughing and ate a lot of their food in the house. James and I had a relationship that was something compared to Martin and Pam's from TV. We joned and played back and forth with smart remarks and laughs. This was every time we came in contact. Because of the extent of our relationship, I called them family. But then, shyt got real and people showed their true colors.

Summer was in full effect and camp had finally started. Brittany was on a trip to Jersey with my cousins Nell and Tiara to visit Tiara's dad. Graham was over our dad's families house, neither one of them would be attending camp only me. I went to camp and one day, we went to six flags and I had a damn ball! I got on everything in the entire park and was just being able to chill with my friends and act like a kid.

Once camp was over I went to B Street to see my aunt and to chill with them for a second. As I walked thru the door I noticed my grandmother. She was a chunky, pretty lady with a beautiful smile and she dressed nicely.

I greeted her with a hug and kiss and immediately went into joke mode. Nothing but a good time was what I had in mind. James was also there and he joined us in the living room for the fun. By the time night fell we were still joking, laughing, and playing. James complained about a back ache when my grandma suggested I massage his back because I'm normally good with things like that. My aunt didn't protest at all. As I did it, we continued having a good time together. None of us had a care in the world.

Normally I was sent home or picked up since my cousins were out of town, but I fell asleep. I was awakened and sent to the room to the left of the apartment. I slept on a mattress on the floor in my camp from that day. As the dark of night turned into the morning sun, I laid on my back with one arm behind my head. The covers slightly were barely on my body when I suddenly felt a slight tug. After the tugging continued for a while, I opened my eyes still have sleep when I asked, "What? You want my belt?"

It wasn't until I opened my eyes completely when I noticed something wasn't right.

I completely woke up and realized that he wasn't trying get a belt, because I didn't have one on. I was wearing a pair of jean shorts and a tank top with a bathing suit under from the 6 flags trip I had the day before.

James was completely naked from head to toe.

He was no little guy. He was 40-something years old and weighed about 230 or 240 pounds. In that moment, I felt like he was going to hurt me, rape me, and kill me. I sensed it. I don't know how, but I did. So, I panicked and tried to run. I immediately slid back to the top of the mattress so I could run out the door when he ran along the side of the bed to catch me. My back was turned to him, so he grabbed my pony tail and slammed me to the floor. Using his brute strength, he turned me to face him while I was forced to lay on my back.

I screamed for help and cried to the top of my lungs when he came close to my ear and threatened, "you better be quiet or I'll have to kill you!"

He was calm but he was dead ass serious. The look in his eyes told me that he didn't want to take it that far, but if he absolutely had to, he'd take my life without question.

I felt defeated, and had never felt that defeated in my life.

I remember praying and asking God to keep me alive. I thought to myself, *God don't let this man kill me. Make someone believe me. Please let me survive this.* And then, I gave up. I let James do whatever it was he wanted to do. I had no fight left in me. I just wanted to live. James told me right before he swabbed what felt like a ton and Vaseline on my vagina that, "this is what has to be done… no one can ever treat you like I could or would."

I closed my eyes and burst into tears as he raped me as forcefully as he could. As if the fact that he raped me wasn't enough, he had sex with a minor - and to make it even worse, his whole fuckin niece. The more James shoved his dick inside of me, he began to get more and more aggressive. The more aggressive he got the tighter his hand got around my neck, which made me cry even harder. He had sex with me for what seemed like forever and from that point on I knew right then that my life had changed. He took a piece of me that I didn't give to him or anybody else. He stole my sanity. My virginity. My body.

When he finally finished, James got up to wash the remnants of my blood off of his body. Me being the person I am, I took that opportunity to try to run away.

The only thing I ran into was even more disappointments.

When I got to the door it was locked from the inside. This meant that in order to get out, I needed a key to unlock the door. This made me I cry even more; I couldn't believe the shyt that was happening to me. I truly couldn't make sense of it all.

James came out the bathroom and said, "Nichole have a seat, let me talk to you." Unlike the first two times, instead of running, I took my ass a seat. In my mind, I just didn't give a rat's ass anymore. *Fuck it, just kill a nigga already*. Once he sat down, this sick fuck preceded to tell that he had been fuckin his two daughters for quite some time. His words were, "What's the use of fucking another nigga when they can fuck me? I give them the world and that's what I been doing. And that can go for you as well. See Nichole the way I see it is you need to be smart and figure out what it is that you want." He smiled and continued. "Is it the new Dickie's? Chuck's? Any shoes that you want? Whatever it is let me know but this offer only stands if you keep this between us."

In my entire mind, for the life of me the only thing that kept coming across my mind was that he's a damn psycho and I needed to get the fuck out of there. *Nichole get yourself out of here but be smart.*

I said, "Listen, you're worried about me telling my mom, you need to focus on whether my will come looking for me. If she does, then there won't be nothing I can say. So just let me go. That way, no habits would be broken, my siblings can get to camp and me too. And everything will be undetected."

He placed the key in the door and told me to hold up. I had breathed a sigh of relief. God heard my prayers. I was in the clear for the moment, but I wasn't safe yet. My eyes watched him intently as he walked to the bathroom. Once he was out of my range of vision, I quickly opened the door and took off.

They were on the third floor so that didn't help my case at all. I made it down the first flight but I damn near fell down the last two flights of stairs. Once I made it to the first floor and hit the door, just before I made it outside, I heard the door slam! I knew he was coming after me and it was life or death. It was literally either me making it a whole block to my mom running, crying, and shaking or he'd snatch me off the street and kill me.

Running towards 35th Street, I ran for dear life to my mother's apartment building. I just so happened to glance over to my left and noticed his town car damn near right beside me. He was holding what looked like a gun in my direction. When I noticed that, I stopped looking at him started to slow up the pace in which I was going. I turned my head by now, scared that he'd pull a trigger at any second. My life flashed before my eyes. My brothers and sister flashed in my mind. Tears ran down my face as I ran to my building door.

There was a key padlock on the building door. I was in so much fear that – despite trying my hardest to stop shaking – I repeatedly put the incorrect code in. It was nothing but the grace of Jesus Christ himself that someone walked right out of my building as I was just about to give up.

With new energy, I raced through the hallway, fighting through tears that blurred my vision. The sound of my cry bounced of the hallway. I could barely get my house keys into the apartment door.

Luckily my mom had not left out to go to work yet; she heard me struggling, so she ran to open the door. I could tell she ran because her footsteps were quick and heavy. The moment she laid eyes on me, she already knew what happened. Maybe it was mother's intuition. Or maybe it was the bloody mess that my clothes had become. Whatever the cause, with anger and revenge in her voice, my mother asked, "Who the fuck touched you Nichole?!"

Paralyzed by everything that happened, fear of retaliation, and a million other things, I didn't say a word for about three minutes. I was still standing in the doorway. The summer heat mixed with the scent of today's actions made me nauseous. My mother walked off, I didn't know why and to be honest, I didn't care. I just stood there.

I looked back up to see my mom standing there with a gun and she asked me again, "who touched you?" Tears were in my eyes when I told her "James" and fell into her arms crying my heart out. My mom called the police mere moments later.

"911, what's your emergency?"

"My daughter was raped!"

"Okay ma'am, is there anyone still in immediate danger? Where is the victim now or are you the victim?"

"No, I am not the victim! I just told you that my daughter was raped! And she is right here we need a damn ambulance… PLEASE!"

"Ma'am, we are going to dispatch EMTs, what's the address?"

"10 35th Street, Washington, DC 20019. Apartment 201."

"Alright ma'am we have the number ten, thirty fifth street southeast apartment two zero one. An ambulance has been dispatched and will be there soon. Please sit tight, help is on the way."

My mom slammed the phone down in anger. She turned toward me. I was still crying, balled up on the living room couch holding a pillow. She looked at me and shook her head. I could tell by the look in her eyes that her heart was broken. She felt bad for me – she was actually hurting for me. She didn't touch me or say too much after that.

Five minutes later the police and ambulance showed up, then we hea.

"It's the police ma'am." My mom jogged to the door. Once the police were let in, the questions immediately started to be thrown at me. I even noticed one of the officers writing down everything I said on a yellow note pad. The more they, talked the more questions they asked. The more questions they asked, the more incoherent I became. The voices became muffled and quieted until I eventually didn't hear anything at all.

My body was consumed with so much emotion that I got light headed and dizzy. I literally lost control of myself. I started to throw up. I stumbled to the bathroom, being caught by walls whenever my knees got weak. When I was in the bathroom and cleaned myself up I heard a knock at the bathroom door. My mom said through the door, "Nichole. The police said don't take a shower, don't change your clothes or bother anything that could be evidence."

I didn't respond, but my mom knew I heard her. She was strong and wise, so she was able to channel her feelings into creating a solution for my situation. I, on the other hand, I was disgusted, angry, sad, emotional, and confused. Who did I wrong to deserve this? What did I do? Was I a sin or two over my limit? Did I not love my mom and dad enough? Was this some type of sick lesson? All I wanted to do was get in the shower and wash away all my sins. I cried some more. At that point, I thought there was nothing left in me. My body proved otherwise.

I mustered all the strength and walked toward the ambulance that, of course, had to be right in front of my damn building. Then it was two cop cars damn near blocking the street off. I felt embarrassed and exposed. It seemed like the random people that was around or in the facility knew what was going on. The stares of the few guys out there made me feel invaded, and it terrified me. The fact that a man had the power – and not to mention the advantage of size, weight, and height – to force me to do just about anything to me he wanted, when he wanted and how he wanted made me feel even more shameful. I took two steps and got on what I hoped would be my last ambulance ride.

EMT's were checking my vitals and shining lights in my eyes when my mom noticed that James was following the ambulance.

My heart instantly started to beat fast and sweat beads formed on my forehead. I couldn't believe that he was actually following us. We were going fast because the sirens were blazing like it was a state of emergency or something. The entire ride, I was hyperventilating and felt genuine fear. It wasn't as bad as the rape itself, but it was just as fuckin bad. I legit thought that he would catch up to us and try to kill us or something. These thoughts crossed my mind until the ambulance pulled up to the hospital.

I was being wheel chaired up to what I guess was a rape victim unit because, judging by the looks on some of these girls' faces, I could tell we were all here for the same reason. Unbeknownst to me, I had no idea of what I was getting ready to endure... taking blood, vitals, blood pressure, urine samples... you name it. Not to mention the endless medicine I had to take. I was told that the medicine was to make me throw up any viruses or infections that I came in contact with. First of all, I hated throwing up – I would sweat profusely, couldn't breathe, and it felt like I was bring up my soul. The pelvic exam, I hated this for obvious reasons. On any other occasion, I loved this process but today I felt like I didn't ever want no one near my vagina again. Then, there was the moment of truth – the part where they find out if I was really raped. It felt like people only really cared about that part. I didn't understand why. I would never lie about something so serious, I mean damn! A bitch could have died!

"Open your legs, put your feet in the braces here," the doctor said to me. It was a few of them around, or maybe they were nurses. I didn't care. I just wanted to go. Next thing I know, something entered me that made my eyes tear up. I was having a hard time trying to figure it what actually bothered me the most: was it the fact that I was hurting and burning and shyt, or the fact that the lady doctor pulled my mom to the side and was whispering something to her off to the side of the room. In my mind, the first thing I thought was that I had AIDS, herpes, or needed surgery to fix my vagina or something.

Suddenly my mom started to cry.

I started to sweat.

The doctor walked back over to me hesitantly; she paused for a second before she spoke. I looked at her intently as my heart raced, anxiously waiting for what was at the tip of her tongue.

When she spoke, she simply gave me directions for my vagina to heal. The doctor explained to me, "As a result of what you have just been through, your insides were hanging out. You also had a rip at the bottom of your vagina, near the anus." My head hung down. I was disappointed in myself. I wanted to turn back the hands of time. Why didn't I see this coming? The only thing left to do was to go finally go talk to my Aunt Nette. She appeared to be hurt, broken, and betrayed. At the time, I really didn't know what to say or how to comfort her. I was never a hugger – I was a strong, stubborn female who never liked showing people any weakness. So, I did the only thing I could think of – which was to apologize to her. I knew from her perspective that what she was going through was different, but don't get me wrong, you can't compare the two. As I walked up to her I was hesitant because I didn't know what to expect. To my surprise, I hugged her and apologized. Unknowingly, that was our last affectionate interaction.

For the next couple of weeks, I was trying to readjust to life. There were days where I was just uncomfortable for no reason at all. There were days where I hurt other people's feelings to protect my own. My relationship with my dad just wasn't the same as it used to be. To make things worse, my mom and I were like estranged lovers or some shyt . We were always arguing. Our life and conversations were reduced to two things: "GET OUT!" or "COME HOME!"

Throughout everything that was going on in my life, there was one person who kept me smiling. This guy named Oliver. I met him during my 9th grade year and we were still talking as we entered our 10th grade year. He stood like 6'1 and reminded me of the guy Chris from the rap group Young Guns. His frame was thick with a brown skin complexion. Hugging him felt like hugging a teddy bear. We had a real strange relationship, but when it came to us, what was understood didn't need to be said. Oliver was starting to be the love of my entire life. I went over his house damn near every day. We spent so much time together just hanging out and talking. Oliver was one of the funniest niggas I knew – there was never a dull moment. The thing I enjoyed the most was that we could talk about any and everything.

Even a year later, it had proven to be really hard for me to form new relationships and bonds with people because of what I had gone through... but for some reason Oliver made me comfortable. Well, at least comfortable enough to confide in him about certain things. So of course, we had the conversation about the rape. The fact that I had to explain that to another man was hard enough, but waiting for a reaction was harder. The court date was coming up and quite frankly I was scared is hell. I hadn't seen James since the rape and I wasn't sure about how I was going to feel coming in contact with him again. My emotions at that point were changing – I went from being sad, hurt and confused to angry, edgy, and wanting revenge. For some reason, it was always a downhill battle for me once I form hate in my heart for you because there is no telling what I'll do or say.

THE COURT DATE

Today was the most humiliating day of my life. I had to look the bastard in the face who took my virginity from me – the muhfucka who changed my life indefinitely. The man who took it upon himself to take what didn't belong to him, without permission, was gonna soon to be standing right in front of my face and it ain't shyt I can do. Accompanied by my mother, who appeared to be ready for war, we walked to our side of the court house where the plaintiff and the family sit. It was one of the coldest feelings ever to find out where your family's loyalty lies. My grandma didn't show up; I'm assuming that she didn't want to have to pick a side. In my head I was like, *okay whatever.* Then the biggest shocker of them all was to look to the right only to see my Aunt Nette sitting with the enemy. A rapist. Her husband. It was a full house to the right of me, filled with his family and friends who showed up in full support of a child molester. That proved to me that the apple didn't fall far from the tree. Every last one of these human beings are crazy and need help.

His confession before everyone was a shocker because last time I heard, the police said he wasn't talking. This probably gave these dummies some hope until he dropped the bomb that no one was expecting. The truth, but following his sick truth he fell into an apologizing mood. He tried to play the sympathy card. I couldn't do anything but stare and shake my head. His apology spoke volumes because he apologized to everyone but his wife – the one who's sitting there backing him in his asshole moment, the person whom he just recently married and said "I do" to. I mean, how sick do you have to be to do some shyt like that? I guess it don't really matter because now he can be someone's sick bitch in jail, cause we all know what they do to niggas in jail that touch children. Needless to say, he was found guilty. His sentencing was scheduled for another day.

My mother got up first. Before she left, she looked to her right and walked out. I followed right behind her. In the car, all my mother did was cry silently as we were on our way home. My dad called while my mom was driving and he was asking to speak to me. For some reason, I didn't want to entertain the phone call. It was like this for a few weeks now. I was starting to realize that I didn't really want to be near any man by myself, nor did I want to talk to one. I knew I was hurting him, but it wasn't my fault that I had these feelings. I felt really bad about it and I wish it was different, but at that particular point in time, a man didn't have nothing coming from me.

* * *

Now that school had started, I had a little bit more to focus on. I got to see Oliver almost every day, which took my mind off a lot of my struggles that I was dealing with. School was a breeze for the most part so I had no complaints there. I had my days where school would just blow me and it made me want to jump, trip up, and knock my own two front teeth out... but I just had regular teenage problems with boys and my friends. On my way to one of the classes I had, I always ran into this lady who, for the life of me, I could never remember her damn name. She would always tell me that I look like this man and we share the same last name. She told me this a hundred times but this particular time, I fed into her convo. Not sure why, but I did.

Long story short she asked me to come to church with her and I told her nah I'll pass, I'm not a morning person. I wasn't lying but I also wasn't with that shyt either for obvious reasons. Walking home from school, I was thinking about that lady and our conversation and decided that I was gonna inquire about some things once I got home. That thought was quickly forgotten when a car drove past blasting I Need a Soldier by Destiny's Child. That was my song, so I slightly sang along with their radio until the music and the car faded away. By then I was walking up to my building. We were living literally two or three buildings over from 10 35th Street – the building where I was staying before I got raped. I was checking my phone as I walked up to put my key in the door. It was around 4:30 and my mom wasn't due home until about 6:30 or 7:00, so I just chilled until then.

"What's up Neise?" I said as my mom walked through the door. I used to play with her sometimes and call by her first name and she'd always would say, "Okay now, Nichole." I would wave her off and finish what I had to say. I walked into her room as she was starting to undress and just continued to have casual conversation until I finally got the courage to ask her the question that had been running through my mind all day. I quietly asked, "Ma... is daddy my biological father?"

"What made you ask me that?"

"I asked because this lady at my school, don't ask me her name because I don't have the slightest clue... we just run into each other every other day... but she told me I looked just like this man at her church and we share the same last name and ma get this... he a preacher!" I fell out laughing, balled up on the bed getting what I would call one of the best laughs in my life when I noticed her ass wasn't laughing. My laughter subsided quick. My mind started to put things together. The conclusion I was coming to was that it must be some truth to this story. One thing I was sure of in that moment was that the man who I called daddy all of these years was not my father. But the million dollar questions were who the hell was my father and why in the hell didn't I get the memo. If I had to put my life on the line, I was gonna find out. Starting right now with the source – my mother.

She sighed and stared at me. "I was gonna tell you once you've gotten a little older when I felt like you could handle it. He never wanted you to know, your father wanted to change your last named on plenty of occasions but I ruled against that because I wanted to tell you first."

"The most crazy thing is you've done worse. You left a man, your husband, and inconvenienced everyone but yourself and I handled that great... so what made you think that I couldn't have handled that situation? What was I not entitled? Once again you think about yourself! What if I would have gone with her? What if she would have brought him to me – because she was dead serious about me seeing and meeting this guy. I would have never treated him differently. That man was here for me and did everything for me, smh. It's cool, ma."

As I was walking to the exit to her room, she stopped me and asked a dumb ass question. I stopped but I never turned around. I blew my breath and could have rolled my eye balls out of my head and into the damn street I was so annoyed. My mother asked me, "So why are you just mad at me? You should be mad at him too, but nooo you would never be mad at your precious daddy, right? Man get out of here." She was angrily putting on her house clothes.

"You have to be joking, right?" I turned around to face her. "To be honest, I'm not mad at him. Why should I be? That man never owed me anything – you did. It shouldn't have been up to him to tell me I'm *technically* your child. He simply had permission to be my father, which he's great at. And it's not about me being mad, it's about me being in the know… not being caught off guard and getting involved in another avoidable situation."

I turned around to walk away but this time with no intentions of going back in the room with her. Little did she know, I was pissed at my father, too… but only because I didn't expect this from him. This nigga told me everything else under the sun, but left that out. Funny thing is, I would bet my life that his reason for not telling me had to be revolving around my mother and her feelings and shyt. My father didn't care what was going on, everything always went in my mother's favor. She always got her way.

With my mind racing and emotions on the rise, I came to the solution that I was never gonna speak of this topic ever again or tell him that I know. I just was convinced that I would never get a fair hand of cards to play.

Oliver and I were on the phone a couple of days later having a good ol' time when he ended the conversation saying that he was coming over. I was so pressed! This guy could give me butterflies and he was no where near me. My phone could ring and before I would answer I would act all stupid and shyt and my sister would grin and roll her eyes in disgust like she always did. He would have me doing all kinds of stupid things that would have my mother wilding out easily. I bought a cordless phone that I unplugged during the day and plugged up at night and cut the ringer off just to be able to talk to him. My mother wasn't having that talk on the phone all night shyt on a school night or any night.

Too bad for her, but I was real determined to talk to my lil boo.

It was 7:00, so I decided to try to find a reason to have to go down stairs so I could see him and not be bothered. The good thing was that when her boyfriend was over our house or on the phone with her, you could literally commit murder. Luckily for me, that ass was on the phone so I was pressed. I peeked into her room and let her know I was washing clothes. She waved me off. I laughed and headed down stairs.

My mother wasn't a bad mom. It was just that I honestly think she missed out on most of her life because she got married very early and they had a hell of an age difference by twenty something years. So, she was really starting to enjoy living her life. Luckily for her, she didn't have no babies; we were old enough to fend for ourselves, which was fine by me.

I got down stairs and gave Oliver a hug and we sat across from each other with me being on the washer and him being on the dryer. We shared small talk and plenty laughs. I don't know what it was about him but I couldn't help but feel weird around him. It was a good thing though. Anytime he would touch me, I would get chills. We still weren't having sex... he was just really sweet towards me. I never understood why he never made a pass at me. I wasn't worried though. The anticipation was in his favor for whenever that day came. We heard the door open to the building and close but I didn't think anything of it because if anyone was coming to my house, it would be my mom's boyfriend. I continued on with my conversation.

A presence entered the door way to the laundry room.

I quickly jumped down at the sight of my father. By this time, we had started having phone conversations because the effects of the traumatic experience I've gone through. At the same time, I don't know why I jumped down as if I was doing anything, but the only thing I could think to say was, "What are you doing here daddy?" I was trying to play it cool, but it was an epic fail because he went the fuck off. For the life of me I didn't understand why. Only thing I thought to respond with was, "Daddy he is only my friend!"

When I was at the point where I felt like I wasn't getting anywhere, I ran upstairs annoyed, tired, upset, and over everything. Once I made it into my house, I ran straight to my room with my mother screaming "What's the matter with you?!" I ignored her.

For some reason, I felt like under my bed was the only place I could go to get away from all the crazy that was going on. My front door slammed and I heard footsteps getting closer to my room. I felt someone sit on the bed following a series of questions.

My father's voice angrily said, "What is your problem? Who the hell is that boy? I told you I'm not for the shyt with these lil boys!"

"You're not my father," I yelled. That's all I could think of saying. Judging from the silence I could tell I hurt his feelings.

I felt bad. I really didn't mean to hurt him, but I was just tired and sick of everything at the point. I laid under the bed and cried until he eventually stood up and left. About 30 minutes after he left, I got in my bed to go to sleep.

Then, my phone lit up. When I answered, it was Oliver to my surprise, I was sure he was never gonna fuck with me again due to my daddy's actions. He was simply calling me to check on me. I updated him and got off the phone because I really just wanted to go to sleep.

* * *

We got word that the last court date was coming up — which was the sentencing. I was really curious to find out if our legal system was honestly gonna make him pay for what he did.

I was nervous as shyt.

Approaching the court room all I felt was nausea and dizziness. This was to me the most important day. I wasn't sure if I ever had entertained the possibility that he may walk free, able to breathe the same air I did, and still have access to me. All my thoughts were flooding my mind giving me a really bad headache.

"All rise for the judge," the bailiff yelled, alerting everyone that court was in session. The judge sat down and immediately began. He wasn't known for playing games.

"In the ruling of James Johnson, I hereby sentence ten years with a chance of parole, with time served counting towards your sentence." My mother was outraged because she told me it wasn't like he turned himself in — they caught him literally trying to cross the Mexican border. What the fuck? I wonder who gave him that dumb ass idea with a warrant. I guess it didn't matter now. Maybe my mom just felt like that wasn't enough time for the crimes he committed... but it was good enough for me long as he was the fuck away from me!

With that being behind me, things were starting to look up, appearing to seem normal for once. And I needed that.

I was on the phone with my friend Dimples talking about these guys that we met at the mall when I overheard a conversation going on in my living room. I quickly hung up on Dimples to listen because it sounded pretty serious judging by the tone and how thick the air was. I heard my mom's boyfriend say, "I'm not leaving my wife. I know what I told you, but I changed my mind. After all... I never told you to leave your husband."

Straight bullshyt is what that was. You can tell that his wife got to him. Maybe threatened him in some way, shape, or form. Shyt, I even wondered if the same lady that wrote my dad wrote to her, too. I didn't know for sure, but what I did know was that what he was saying was bullshyt. It pissed me off because him and I had conversations before. He loved her – I mean he LOVED her – so I couldn't believe he was doing this after he fucked our life up. I stepped out where he could see me. My mother glanced at me, didn't say anything, then looked back towards him. He gave her a look that was supposed to signal her to dismiss me but she didn't. As he went to part his lips my mother punched him dead in his mouth and said, "Get the fuck out and don't ever contact me again."

I just thought to myself *'my mom is a nut case.'* Chuckling to myself, I smirked and walked away to watch TV because that shyt was crazy. That punch had hurt my feelings. And wait... married?! I was trying to figure out if she knew this before or was this news to her. Shyt, it was damn sure news to me. Man, this was some Maury stuff right here. He was sitting there wondering how he was about to go home to his wife with a fucked up lip. I don't know, he better tell her ass he got robbed... before I knew it, I was chuckling again before cutting the TV on and searching for something to watch.

2005

At this point, I'm sixteen now and coming into my own. I changed just a little and I wasn't the same old little Nichole no more. I was back to normal – well as normal as I was going to get because of my past – but things had gotten better with my bonds and my relationships and friendships. I met this guy named Scrappy. He was short and a chocolate drop. He had the prettiest smile and he always dressed nice is hell. I had already lost my virginity, officially that is, to Oliver. But shortly following that event, things kind of changed. Oliver and I still talked... we loved each other... but at this time we were on and off. Because of the inconsistency, I met someone. Scrappy and I used to kick it all the time especially because my friend Dimples was talking to his friend so we all would kick it together sometimes. I was feelings him a lil and I was cool with that. I could deal with the less complicated aspect of this new bond I was building. Things were finally starting to look up.

I ended up going through a few thing with my mom and she put me out, so that forced me to have to go live with Scrappy. It had its pros and cons but it was cool. I fell in love with his mom; her name was Angel. She really took a liking to me and never gave me no hassle, even if it came down to her son. One day Scrappy and I was arguing and she hit him in his nose with a broom. Even when our relationship got rocky, she didn't pick a side; she simply said what was right was right and what was wrong was wrong. I always respected her for that because I learned a lot from her. He was accepted into my family as well.

The relationship between me and Scrappy started to feel like a marriage because we did everything together – whether we wanted to or not.

In September, I remember crushing food and feeling sick but it was kinda cold so I chalked it up to me maybe about to come down with a cold. One day, one of my friends went to the Planned Parenthood on Minnesota Avenue and dragged me along. I was only supposed to be there for support, but ended up taking an STD, HIV, and pregnancy test because I was bored. I didn't have anything else to do, so fuck it, why not, right?

To my surprise, the doctor came back in making a face that was making me uneasy. For some apparent reason, I also thought the worst again. I actually blurted out, "OMG I got AIDS!"

She said, "No you don't have AIDS. However, you are pregnant." My friend and I were both looking like we saw a ghost. The doctor said, "I'll give you a second," and stepped out. I was pressed – not about the father, hell no – I just always wanted to be a mom so I can give my kid the world and love them and for once someone to love me.

The doctor walked back in and said, "So is this a wanted pregnancy?" I responded, "I don't know but we will see." I thanked her and we left. During my whole ride to Paradise I kept catching myself smiling at the news I just received. U6 was the bus I was on and it was hella crowded. I sat to the back of the bus by the window to the left with the window slightly open, the cool July breeze hitting my face. The bus felt like it was riding smoother. The people looked happier that's how happy I was. At this point I could have gave a shyt about Scrappy or anyone else it was about me and my baby. I rang the bell as I was approaching Justice Court and the bus came to a complete stop. I hoped and walked to the building. Of course, when I got home he wasn't there so I could bet my life that he was out there being a nigga.

I started cleaning up and looking for something to eat when he suddenly walked through the door.

I simply stated, "I'm pregnant."

"What, you pregnant?"

"Yea, pregnant."

"How you know?"

"Nigga! From the doctor."

"I'll be back."

He didn't seem mad or happy, but he ran out the door. It was hard to read him. It didn't matter though because he didn't have a choice in the matter. I was having my baby and honestly his only choices were to either be there or not, which, to keep it a hundred, I didn't give a fuck either way. I also wasn't gonna hold it against him. It wasn't about him. It was about me. This moment, as far as I was concerned, was mine, and I wasn't going to let him or anyone else get in my way. This included my mother, because she was next on my list to tell. She was capable of getting on my nerves, and I wasn't here for it.

After I finished my food I got myself together and headed to my mother's house.

* * *

I knocked on the door and waited for what felt like forever. My mother always took two hundred and seven days to open the door. I heard her skipping and shyt and shook my head. I got in and was wondering where my sister Brittany was. I was definitely trying to tell her the good news, too! She was probably with that ugly girl. I headed to the other side of the apartment noticing it was really quiet in my mother's room. I asked her, "Ma what you in here doing laughing?"

"Girl shut up. I was on a phone call, hence the note pad on the bed. And don't you be playing with me like that," she said, slightly chuckling.

"Sooo, guess what?" I cheesed so hard. I couldn't help myself.

"What, girl?"

"You're about to be a grandma! I'm pregnant!"

"...and you happy about that?"

In my mind, I'm like... *you know what... Why can't anyone ever be happy for me – why must everyone act like dicks? I already see where this is going. I'm about to dead this whole conversation. I'm not for anyone or they craziness. I'll just let Angel talk to her, so I need to hurry up and tell her.* "Nah ma, it's okay. Forget I said anything. I'll handle it." I rolled my eyes and started walking out the house.

"Thank you."

I don't know what she thought I meant by "I'll handle it," but I was keeping my kid. I rushed home so that I could tell Angel, so I hoped she was not sleep. I ran upstairs and walk straight through the door. Angel always left her door unlocked. I found her sitting at the table eating and she was by herself. So, I took a seat and got straight to the point. I felt like I been doing that a lot lately.

"Angel, I went to the doctor today and found out I was pregnant."

As soon as I was done talking, her phone rung. I was so annoyed because that was bullshyt that right there. The Devil was trying to ruin my life. I sat there for what felt like my whole damn life. The suspense was killing me. All types of thoughts were entering my mind... and if she took the news hard, I would be uncomfortable with continuing to live there. Finally, she was off the phone

"So, you keeping it?"

"Yea."

"So it don't matter what I think. That's ya'lls baby. Have you told Scrappy yet?"

"Yea."

"What he say, girl?"

"Nothing. He said he'll be back and he left out."

"Well did you eat? You know you need to feed that baby."

I laughed out loud, "I know, I'm about to eat now."

And just like that the conversation was over. Nice and smooth, no pressure, just a conversation. This is why I fuck with Angel. She just too cool for school and loving the fact that a baby was growing inside of me. I swore everything about my life was making me happy. Nothing bothered me. Because this was my first pregnancy, I wasn't really aware of everything I probably should have been aware of. Some would have argued that's why I shouldn't have had a baby but guess what? Nichole was having a baby. Over the course of the next couple months or so, Scrappy and I started to have our issues but they weren't nothing too serious. We were still us for the most part.

One night we were having sex and as soon as we were done I started to bleed. No one informed me about miscarrying, so I didn't know what that meant. I didn't do anything. I just bled. I was bleeding for almost seven days now, during that seven day period my mom called a meeting between Scrap and his mom, and me and my mine. I was scared, and just wanted to die.

THE MEETING

"Hey Angel, I'm Niese, how are you?"

"I'm good thanks. So what's going on?"

"I'm trying to get your take on this whole baby situation."

"Well the way I see it is, if they want to have a baby that's on them. I'm not against it, but I'm not for it either."

I decided that my voice needed to be heard. "Ma why can't you just ever be supportive and why must you be so negative?"

Angel stepped in. "Nichole, that's still your mother. You need to chill."

My mother's attitude was about to come out. I already felt it. "Don't tell her nothing. That's why she not here now because of her damn mouth," she looked straight into my eyes and dared me to start arguing with her.

"I don't even want to talk about it no more, I'm good," I said as I got up and walked away. At this point in my life, I was done. It just seemed like nothing but negativity was around me and it was never gonna get any better. As I was headed back to Angel's house I started to ache in my stomach. Now although I had been bleeding all week, I never felt like this. The pain was something that came and gone, but it was one of those feelings that would have you balled up in a corner crying your heart out. I didn't really want to move once this feeling came about because with every ounce of pain that shot thru me I knew my baby was dying. I felt it. I wasn't home for more than 30 minutes before I was heading out to the hospital. The first person I called was my mom. Even though we disagreed, she had my back and would go to war for me. So it was only natural that she came running at the news. She met me in front of the abandoned houses right on B Street and 37th where I was standing at the bus stop.

I was forced to ride the bus, or at least I thought I was gonna ride the bus because Angel had the car and she wasn't home yet. Scrappy of course was nowhere to be found. Approaching Washington Hospital Center in NW, my mom was rushing to find parking and God knows it took forever because she always wanted to be cheap, with her cheap ass. Experiencing heavy bleeding I was completely covered in blood from the waist down. Walking through the doors of the ER, you would have thought that the nurses or doctors would have catered to me. They didn't.

The lady said that my condition wasn't life threatening, and there were a few people in front of me. "You have to be patient and bare with us; people was here waiting just like you. We will be with you soon, sit tight. Okay?"

My mother lost her shyt! "What the hell you mean it's not a life threatening situation! I mean come the fuck on now, she got so much blood on her it look like she been shot! This shyt don't make no sense. Y'all have muhfuckas sitting around here dying and y'all in here not doing shyt! Nichole let's get the fuck out of here before you fuck around and die in here!"

I did as I was instructed. I followed my mother back to the car but as time went on my pain worsened and I bled out more… so much that my mother made me sit on some newspaper. It was September, so it was pretty cool outside and I must say the cool air wasn't helping me with my pain. In fact, it caused me to shiver against what felt like labor pains. She told me she loved me (but not enough for me to fuck up her seats). I loved my mother. Pulling up to yet to another ER in a different area, Georgetown was the hospital of my mom's choice. She informed me that it was one of her favorite hospitals other than GW.

As soon as I appeared in the opening doors they rushed to me with a wheel chair and attended to me quickly. This was now my favorite hospital. I was whisked away to some unit within the hospital where I ended up with a mask over my face counting back from one hundred. I never even felt myself go to sleep.

I remember waking up in pain and wondering what the hell even happened. I woke up to faces that weren't there before, Angel and Scrappy was in attendance to support, but honestly it made my day because I could have bet bread that the nigga didn't give a shyt about me or this baby.

I found that I had surgery for them to remove the remains of the baby because that was in fact what was causing the pain. That surgery was called a DNC. They issued me plenty of pain meds with instructions on how to take care of myself to prevent infections and things like that. To my surprise ma dukes asked me to come back home and I accepted. Following the discharge papers, I started to look for my clothes that my mom sent for because the ones I came in was thrown in the trash because of the blood. We talked for a few on the ride home just long enough for her to inform me that she had something really important to talk about and that it was sensitive. I have no clue on what this conversation entails but I would soon find out. We weren't far and before we know it we were home.

I took a shower and got comfortable when I heard my name being called. I already knew what she wanted and that was to have the talk. I headed straight for her room and laid across the bed when I simply said, "Wassup, ma?"

"So I know it's been a few years and I know you might not want to talk about it or even talk to me about it but I have to ask."

I started chuckling to myself because I'm like oh lord what the hell are we about to talk about, because all I know is I do not want to be mad I'm too damn tired.

"Ask what ma?"

"Do you think that Nette had anything to do with what happened to you?"

I paused because I made sure I took the time out to actually hear what she was asking me. Honestly, I had already thought that because of the way my aunt moved after the rape happened. We didn't have a good relationship at all, we even was going to fight a couple times. I felt as if she felt that it was my fault and she acted as if I fucked her husband. I tried to put myself in her shoes, but I always felt that even if that was the case, he still is attracted to a minor. Consensual or not, it's not a good look. He is a got damn child molester and did something with her own flesh and blood.

"Seriously ma, I replayed that situation in my head two hundred and seven times and it never made sense. I tried and I tried to try to figure out was there anything I could have done differently. Even went is far as to blame myself because normally I go home. But not this not ma, I was able to stay. Crazy thing is that's not the fucked up part ma, what got me was when I woke up completely I couldn't believe that I was in the house alone by myself, and left alone with James at that. Ma you already know how aunt Nette operate anytime I was left alone if I was at grandma house she would call and tell me I would have to go until grandma got back home and if I was down her house I had to leave when she left out." I furrowed my eyebrows as I continued. I was starting to get angry.

"I talked to Nell and he had told me an ear full. He explained that his mom told him that I came on to James and that I'm fast, I broke up a happy home, I was a liar, so forth and so on. I mean it has to be love right ma, right? I don't know what planet I have to be on to stand behind a known rapist or accused rapist – especially when I don't have all the details." I looked at my mom's hurt face.

"So yea, I been thought about that. Again, I replayed the events over and over even the actual act of it all just in case I missed something. For a long time I hated myself because in the moment of the rape I gave up, it felt too close to consent. I should have fought more, I should have screamed louder but I didn't. I could have stood my ground but I gave in. I allowed another human to have mental, physical, and emotional control over me. I allowed another man to put the fear in God in me, to do the opposite of everything that you guys instilled in me. I should have died first. I should have died if it meant giving him the power over me."

At the moment, all my mother did was hang her head down. You could see the devastation all over her face. For the first time my mom was at a loss and I have never seen her like this before. She hesitated before she responded to anything I said. Before she spoke she wiped her face as tears welled up in her eyes. "Nichole… I'm going to get down to the bottom of this. I'm going to go talk to momma and Nette. I'm going to find out."

"Ma, it's no need. The way I see it is bad things happen to bad people. As far as I'm concerned, maybe this was the way things were supposed to be or the way things were supposed to happen. Clearly I didn't have a choice in the matter. So yes, I do feel as though I have been set up.

However, there is nothing that I can do but play the hand I was dealt and play those cards to the best of my ability."

Now in my head, I know exactly what I was saying and I also knew the details that supported my thoughts. I decided to keep those details to myself and not reveal them to anyone and that included my mother. I knew that if I gave her my real thoughts with certain details it will make her push for counseling. I didn't need it. If it wasn't one thing that I was good at it, it was taking my thoughts, breaking them down, and putting them into perspective. Figuring out the root or source of where they came from. Also figuring out how they play out in my everyday life and how my mental state or thoughts effect my everyday decisions.

I wanted to tell my mom the changes that I realized as a result of the rape. I became a very sexual being. Sex became my first line of defense and my first line of communication in my relationships. To me, sex was nothing more than a bunch of physical actions and a series of emotions. Now, some people go by actions speak louder than words. Others go by communication is key. A few may operate on trust. So with that, I feel like from the rape I learned so much more from the tragic events I endured. I've learned to look deeper into people's actions – whether it's in their worst moments or you're in your worst moments. James showed so much more to me in that moment. His actions explained a lot. They explained and also let me know that this was thought about before it actually happened. Basically premeditated.

During the actual act, he took his time waking me and starting the whole process, which showed me that he cared on the emotional side. He didn't want to scare me. When he swabbed me with the Vaseline, that let me know he wasn't trying to hurt me. Talking to me was him looking for consent and trying to remain in control (him threatening to kill me). James actively having sex with me the way he did showed enjoyment – it was wanted on his part. With him feeling the need to explain, convince, and bribe was him subtly letting me know he wanted sex to continue.

Now I also came to the conclusion that maybe on his part he thought that feelings were mutual because of how we interacted with each other – Martin and Pam relationship that I mentioned before. Maybe it was that back rub from the night before that my grandma told me to give him. So now being a sexual being works for me.

After having thought everything through, I headed out for some food. While on the way to my grandmother and aunt, my mother and I joked and played around. That was something that we hadn't really done in a while. It was because of our estranged relationship; it was rocky and we had more downs than ups at this point. Also, add the fact that I was always put out, really didn't feel loved, and only felt a connection with my mom during a tragedy. I rerally basked in the moment because it was rare with her. In the drive thru of McDonalds, I got my famous number 7, the McNugget meal and a sprite that literally touched my soul. I asked my mother, "Do we really have to go and get down to the bottom of something that happened 2 years ago?"

Her silence meant yes.

As we pulled up to the building at 3600 Ely Place, where both my aunt and grandmother stayed at the time, we were trying to find a parking space but again my mother is so irritating because she acts like we have to be parked right in front of the door. I reached for the handle of the car when my mother told me to hold up. She wanted me to sit in the car to finish eating my food so that she had time to get a feel of how the situation was about to play out. She said she'll call me when to come up.

I'm sitting in the car eating just about to take a sip of my soda when my phone rang. It's been about 45 minutes and the radio was blowing me and so was this ugly boy that was staring at me through the windshield. The car was facing the Stone Ridge Apartments. On the second ring, I answered only to hear yelling and harsh breathing which gave me the impression that my mom was running. I asked, "Are you ok? What's wrong? What's going on?"

"Girl these muhfuckas is a trip! They fuckin jumped me!"

The phone abruptly hung up.

I was pissed! I was gonna fuck some shyt up once I got upstairs. I couldn't believe that they had the audacity, the heart, to even play with my mother. *It's cool though, cause I'm tagging that ass – anyone who want this work! Women, children, babies, grandmas, aunts, cousins, female or male, watch!*

All I could do was jump out the car and head straight to apartment 326. Now, I knew that my mother wasn't in the house because I heard her in the hallway. By the time I got all the way up there, my mom was nowhere in sight. I hit the same hall twice so I headed right back to the car. Coming through the door closest to my grandma's door, I ran back into my mom where she instantly started yelling. "This shyt don't make no sense! I'ma get Nette ass and can you believe that Tiara jumped in and momma sat on me?!"

I chuckled to myself – not at the events, but at the fact she called my grandma that old ass name. What the hell is a momma?! I cracked the fuck up in my head. She was literally the only one in our family that call my grandma that. "Ma are you serious?"

The only person that surprised me with their actions was Tiara. She wasn't capable of shyt. That ass wasn't built to pop a damn balloon, let alone swing on my mother, but that's what's up though. I had something coming for her.

"Nichole, let's get the fuck out of here. You know how they are, they'll get to lying and shyt and I can't get in no trouble or I'll lose my job. Them muhfuckas called the police on me and they jumped me! Nichole I'm serious I don't give a damn about an apology. DON'T EVER BRING YO ASS BACK UP HERE!"

I just shook my head. I wasn't gonna even respond to that because I knew I would be back. As we rode in the car, all I could think about was what I would do once I snuck over there and saw them face to face. Before I knew it, we were pulling back up to my mother's house. I never would say my house even if I was living there, simply because it never felt like home. Soon as I got in the house, I took the best shower I had in a long time. It was a nice, long, hot shower – so hot that my body was red and really soft. I ended up getting sleepy so I laid down in my bed and I drifted off to sleep.

2007

Things were finally looking up; drama seemed to have subsided for a substantial amount of time. And I was loving it. I was 17 and my 18th birthday was right around the corner. I was madly (but stupidly) in love with Oliver. I had my friends but Oliver was it for me. Me and my dad were back together like we used to be. My dad and I never fell off in terms of talking on the phone, but things just wasn't the same after I went through the rape. I just couldn't be around him like that for a while. But I was definitely starting to feel the effects of not having my dad... that unique bond that we shared, that real love hate relationship. That man could irritate me to my soul, but if he called and asked me to ride, I was still down. He could curse me out and afterward would still ask if I needed anything. I thought it was so weird, but that was the homie though. The one person I felt like he loved more than me was my mother. I asked God two hundred and seven times to have my dad to let her go. I mean she left him in 2003, but he never stopped and if I didn't know any better I would think that his love for her grew.

Every conversation between him and I had to start off about my mother and I hated that because she did not love him back. She had moved on again. Even though I never wanted to listen, I did because I felt like he needed an ear. It was January, but he had maybe been living in that particular apartment since December. My dad was living across the street from my mom who had also moved out to Bladensburg, Maryland – right off of the parkway. At times it was convenient, but most times it was just plain annoying. Of course, my mother took advantage of that because every other day was still get the fuck out, and the shyt wasn't considered drama anymore because that was old news. I had gotten used to it, so every other day, I was at my father's house. Hella convenient. The annoying part was when I wasn't put out, it was always 'go ask your father for this,' 'go see if he got that.' For somebody who wasn't fuckin with him, she sure did ask him for a lot.

Anyway, Oliver and I had developed a strong bond and we were like best friends. We never really tried titles because we knew what it was. I saw him every day for the most part, up until February. I signed up for boot camp to go get my life together. I told him about it and he had told me handle my business. Before I was set to go, I literally chilled with everyone I could – well the people I cared about that is.

Brittany, that was my ace boon coon. We pretty much was getting in trouble together now. We told each other everything, lied for each other, snuck boys in through the windows. We had a great bond and I wouldn't change it for the world. That was baby sis though, I would have done anything for her. She was 14 now, so the age difference didn't seem that far off.

My mother hated our relationship… or maybe she didn't… but it seemed like it lol. She swore to the man upstairs that I was a bad influence and that I was taking her down the wrong path. I never understood why because I never would really let her do much. I'm actually very overprotective of her. Despite that, my mother wasn't budging when it came to how she felt. Brittany was smart, real smart, so I didn't have to worry about much. She did good in school, wasn't really doing much at home, so I really didn't understand what ma's problem was.

Graham's ass was in and out. He never really stuck around long. After all, it was a house full of women. And he hated when my mother started drinking. My mom became an alcoholic and we all hated it. Sober mom was cool. Drinking mom turned into the devil herself. She would just go off, and when she did, no one was safe. Police were always called and someone was leaving every time.

One day all of us were at home. Everyone was chilling and my mom came for my lil brother. That was the wrong move because this nigga had an attitude problem. He was in his room when she started to yell and scream. Mommy said one thing that he didn't like and the next thing I know, the blender flew across the room. That attitude trait can be found in pretty much all of us, but the worst of the attitudes can be found in Graham and Wannell. Wannell was the same way in terms of leaving at the first signs of trouble. No bye, no nothing. You'll never see that nigga again for years.

Meanwhile, one day as I was chilling with my sister and her dude, I was introduced to a guy named Double A. I thought he was the cutest thing. He had the prettiest smile and he was an edgy nigga. It was just something about him lol. He was crazy – he did wild shyt I didn't like, like whip his dick out and grab who ever ass he liked. But even that didn't turn me off. It drew me to him. He was younger than me, but I really didn't care about his age because when having conversations with him, he could hold his own. He was driving and I wasn't even driving so I thought that was a plus. Double A was a nigga wit all the hoes, so I never really entertained the thought of a relationship. Spending time with him was keeping me afloat so I was cool with that. We don't even need to mention that Oliver had all my attention.

Waiting for the T18 out Blade was like waiting on Jesus to get to you at the Gate. I was so anxious to get to Oliver. It was like I couldn't get there fast enough. Finally, I arrived at his house and my heart was beating fast and I felt like I had to throw up. Surprisingly the house was empty and it was just him and I.

We went in the room to get comfortable and watch some TV. It was our thing, and endless movie watching was the goal. Sometimes we played around and talked a little – just really enjoying each other's company was all we ever did. In his room, there were pictures covering the wall, nothing but females. 98% of the females was either talking to him or probably having sex with him. I really use to look at this nigga like he was crazy. He always fed me and took care of me while I was around, and I think that's what I got attached to.

BOOT CAMP

February was coming quickly. I was heading off to boot camp soon and I was ready but not really. I was scared because my father didn't want me to go. I think it was because he was diagnosed with a brain tumor and lung cancer last year. Last year, I was living with my dad in a hotel out Suitland briefly when I literally didn't have nowhere to go. He was going on and on about my mother when out of nowhere he was looking like he was seizing and I knew he wasn't because he was still talking. My dad kept repeating, "I'm aight, I'm aight. I'm aight." I looked at him intensely not sure of what the hell was going on, and then he just stopped and went back to normal. I asked him, "What's wrong with you? And don't lie!"

He looked at me before answering. "I'm sick baby."

"What you mean you sick? Sick how?"

"I have cancer."

"Well, have you at least been to the doctor?"

"No!" He shouted. "I'm okay Nichole, leave it alone and don't tell your momma you hear?"

"Maaaan I'm not trying to hear that. You need to go to the doctor. And I am gonna tell my mova because this is dumb. And I promise you if you don't go to the doctor I'll never speak to you again."

My dad just got up and walked outside. There wasn't too many places to go in this little ass hotel room. I quickly called my mother and she was there in no time to my surprise. And so was damn near all of his family trying to see what was going on with my dad.

He was admitted to the to the hospital last year. That's when he fell into a coma. One day we all were a united front at the hospital looking at him sleep. Everyone one by one went to hold his hand one more time before they left. I was one of the last ones – me and my grandmother. Nobody was fucking with them still, but I guess she was there for support. I grabbed his hand and my grandma said, "Nichole, look he smiling." I was so pressed because he was really my first love. Shortly after that he came out of his coma, and he slowly but surely went downhill ever since he started chemo therapy.

Chemo was breaking him down and he wasn't able to really pick himself up after that. I guess he felt the need to tell me how he felt about things that was never spoken about and made sure that I knew he loved me. One of the first topics was rape. He never spoke to me about it but I always knew he felt away about it but I just chalked it to him hurting behind me not seeing him. One of the things that I never knew was that he was heartbroken. He never really knew how to talk to me about it, he cried many nights, and he apologized if I felt that he wasn't there for me. He just wanted me to know that he loved me very much and he tried everything he could to protect me.

I heard everything he said and I believed every word of it. I can honestly say that I needed to hear that. Me and my dad's relationship wasn't always this way. He was so mean to me as a child that on many occasions, my mom had to step in. She never went for that shyt at all. My father would always accuse me of shyt, whether I actually did it or not, I swear I felt like he used to arrange days of the week to beat my ass. He wasn't like that towards my sister and brother. When I would talk to them about it, my siblings would both tell me "nigga cause you be doing stuff!"

They were right though. One day I did something and he slapped me dead in my face. I couldn't even cry because I was shocked. During this heart to heart in the hospital, daddy told me he was mean because he was mad that I wasn't biologically his and that my mom wouldn't let him change my name. It bothered him that sooner or later he would have to tell me and I would change. It was a blessing that we were able to change things and permanently move to a more positive relationship.

Days came and days went, and before I knew it, February was here and I was all packed up and ready to go. I was seriously second guessing the move because I was going to be away for six whole months. Away from my sister Brittany, my daddy, my nigga Oliver, and my friends. I knew that my daddy really didn't want me to go but my mom was pushing me out the damn door. She even paid for all my stuff to go. I could never get too much of anything from her.

Everyone accompanied me to the Armory where I had to go to be picked up and taken to St. Mary's fuckin county. I was really annoyed with being so far away. At this point, all I was concerned with was these weekend passes because

I was trying to know for sure that I was coming home sometimes. I wasn't sure how bad of an experience I was setting myself up for, but I definitely was going because I really wanted things to be different. I really just wanted a consistent place to sleep and eat every day. I was so done with the back and forth.

As I walked in in the Armory, my heart dropped. All I heard was Beyoncé's song, Irreplaceable, blasting through the speakers. All I kept thinking was *damn... I'm probably not gonna even hear no music for a long time*. I had no idea what to expect once I was there. It was a DC program, so I never knew who I would run into – be it good or bad. I had been having a lot on my mind and I needed to clear my head. With my dad being sick, I literally was just waiting for him to pass and I hated that. I hated feeling like I was wishing death but I wasn't. I just was trying to prepare myself for the worst.

As I loaded myself on the bus, a little excitement came over me. I felt a sense of peace. I felt a sense of stability. I literally felt like a brand new person, but I knew that I was going to be missing people before the bus even got down the street. As we pulled up to the facility, the air was different. There was a lot of space... too much space if we want to really talk about it. I noticed three buildings in sight soon as I stepped off the bus. I had to switch from my cute bags that I brought with me to this big, ugly ass, long, army green bag. I was ordered to put that shyt on my back and soon as I hit the ground run! That's exactly what I did, I ran. It seemed like it took me forever to get to the place where I was told I was sleeping.

I was exhausted from running, but I walked into a room full of bunk beds! I was hella irritated because I expected to have my own room. Then on top of that it was like 19 or 20 of us but in the mist of me counting I noticed two people I knew: Taji And Nita. Taji always been bae, and me and

Nita were cool at one point but her and her folks jumped me back in junior high school for what I thought was over a boy.

In boot camp, I got to know a few girls here. Meesha and I birthdays fell on the same day (May 15th). She was a year younger than me. There was another girl who was just a perpetual liar. For the most part, our instructors were cool; of course, there was one lady I didn't care for. I met another lady named Ms. Rudd. I really liked her. She didn't put a lot of pressure on me and she allowed me to use the phone to call Oliver and my dad. They were both pretty much the only people that I had missed other than Brittany. She snuck me DVD's and little snacks and stuff. My dad sent me endless money as if I could spend it. My mom was really only concerned with me wanting to come home early. Little do she know I never wanted to come home. I wanted my own shyt and being here is was my first step.

Family day came around and, to my surprise, I was sooo pressed to see my sister, brother, and my mother. I missed her and hadn't really talked to her since I had been there. I didn't know who else was coming and Oliver said that he couldn't make it, but I missed him like crazy. Family day was only two hours, yet, I was actually nervous because what if they didn't miss me or were already in a bad mood and ruined my day?

I looked through the crowd and scanned the area for my family. For a second, I was getting nervous because I couldn't find them. It would have hurt me if no one showed up. Then I spotted my mother. I knew that flat ass anywhere and them ugly ass curls. Despite all that, her smile could have lit up a room. Her teeth were really straight – her grill was perfect. I starting running over there to her when Graham stepped out from behind her. He walked up to me, grabbed me so tight, picked me up off my feet, and spun me around. He actually missed me. He put the biggest smile on my face. Then my sister gave me a big hug as well. She surprised me with the brand new Beyoncé B-Day CD. Man was there, too. Man was my mother's new boyfriend and she was so pressed for him.

But my daddy was nowhere to be found, I was mad and hurt all at the same time. I asked my mother where he was and she said he couldn't make it and left it at that. When I talked to him a couple of days ago he told me that he was fine. I just figured that my mom rather Man be with her than him, which I guess made sense. The day still managed to turn out great and I was so grateful.

Family day was over and the girls in my barracks had plans for the night.

Illegal plans lol.

We were going to see the boys who were about a two minute walk away from my barracks. We kinda did that often lol we were still girls. All we did was talk of course. We never had the time to do much else. I was looking good too, I gained a lot of weight because I ate three times a day and I ate all of my food including desserts. Peach cobbler was the best, I really didn't know what I was missing. It was first time having it and I didn't plan on making it my last.

July was our final month in boot camp and honestly, I was scared to leave. I felt like I had a little family here. Plus, I really didn't know what to expect once I got home... but I had a couple more days to go. They moved us from off campus because of a technical issue. This mean we lucked up being in a hotel for our last days and that shyt was great!

We all were called for an emergency meeting outside where we had to line up to receive whatever news was to come. The instructor spoke and let us all know that 6 people are going home early for good behavior. I was one of them. So, I was directed to my room to retrieve my things to board. I was told we weren't going the way we came and that we were all riding in separate cars. I really didn't care how I got home, I just wanted to see my father. The whole two hours I was riding back up the road, I was anxious happy. First thing I did was reach for the phone that Ms. Rudd always let me use, but she snatched the phone from me (which I thought was weird) but I didn't fight it. I just sat back. I asked can I call my dad to tell him I'm on the way? She said her phone didn't have no minutes I looked at her as confused as all hell, but again, I just sat back and minded my business.

Pulling up to my mom's apartment out Blade, I ran to drop my bags off so I could run across the street. As I was opening the door I saw the door close again. My sister and brother weren't home so it was just me and my mother. When I looked to my left, I noticed my mother blocking the exit. I asked, "What are you doing?"

"Nichole, you didn't get a free pass for good behavior. I asked for you to come home," she said as she took a long, breathy pause. In my mind I'm like *what type of shyt is she on? Why is she preventing me from leaving?* "Your father passed away yesterday morning on the Fourth of July."

I was speechless. *What she mean dead? He's not dead. She wild as shyt for making some shyt like that up. She always has to say something negative. Always have to ruin a moment I mean damn I just got home, where the food at?* But the longer I stood there, the more my heart broke, the more heated my body got. Although I'm in my own thoughts and silent toward her, I noticed that she never switched up her facial expression.

I knew that face. Her heart was breaking for me again and I knew right then that she was serious. I knew right then my father was dead.

I started to cry because I just knew that I was gonna run over there and break in like I always did. I was going to get on his nerves and he would make me those jail house ass dinners as if he was poor or he been to jail. I just knew I was gonna get the warmest hug and that hard ass kiss he use to give out. I just knew that was going to happen. But not today, or any other day. Ever again.

To make it worse was that on July third, I was watching the fireworks down at St. Mary's sitting on a rock. I wasn't happy because that very morning, I had a dream about my dad dying and mouthing that he loved me. It felt so real that it bothered me throughout the whole day. I called but I didn't get an answer. I never said goodbye. I never got to say I love you or nothing. As far as I was concerned FUCK LIFE because every time I turned around I was screaming FUCK.

"FUCKKKKK!" I screamed with tears flooding my face.

"Nichole, calm down. Take it easy, I know you upset."

"Nah man you did this! If you would have let me see him when I asked, I would have at least said goodbye but no… you was so concerned with me staying away. You only think about yourself!" I walked straight out the door and went to Oliver house. He was the one of the only people who I knew could relate to me and what I was going through. He lost his dad as well, so I hoped he had some idea of how to get through this.

I got to his house and we sat on the floor, it was quiet but he didn't ask me what's wrong. I think he knew already. I mean me and Oliver talked about it before and he for the most part told me that everything will be okay. So he was fully aware of what my dad was going through. Out of nowhere, he asked if my father died. All I could do was cry and I laid on his shoulders. He did whatever he could to keep my mind off of it.

It worked for a while but once it was near time to go to sleep my mind was flooded with memories.

The next week was hard for me and I'm sure it was hard for my siblings. I really didn't spend too much time with them nor had I seen them because I kinda sort of moved in with Oliver and only went home occasionally. I was really trying to figure out why they didn't bury my dad yet. I didn't even know who was taking care of the arrangements because all I heard was that they banned my mother from the funeral. Those people on my dad's side were just evil. They had the game fucked up because Neise ass was going to the funeral.

I remember when daddy told me and Brittany that the doctors gave him a couple of weeks – maybe less to live. This happened during one of my free weekend passes home. This is why I asked to come home because of what he said. I didn't think he was lying because I reacted to what he said, but I think that I was being really optimistic about the whole ordeal. He told me that if nothing else happened, he wanted me and my brothers and sister there next to my mother. He felt like he really didn't care about anyone else being in attendance; he only wanted his kids and his wife. He never stopped referring to her as his wife, I don't think I would've ever heard him call her his ex-wife.

Almost two weeks later, I was surprised that my father was not in the ground yet and I was starting to not understand why. It came off as if they were stalling and I didn't like that; I felt like he should have been treated with a little bit more respect. At the end of the day, though, I didn't know anything. I really had no details of the planning and I just kind of wanted the nightmare to be over.

I had been anxiously awaiting the day of the funeral, but I honestly wasn't ready at all. I wasn't quite ready to say goodbye. Just when I thought I made peace, I quickly realized that I hadn't. My dad was everything to me at this point. We had our ups and downs, but we were us and I knew that I was gonna miss him dearly. Walking up to the casket, I was approaching it really slowly. For some reason, I didn't want to see him like that until I got a sense of relief when the person in the casket looked nothing like my dad. The guy in that casket was two days past dark. He was really frail-looking and he just wasn't my dad and I stuck with that. I only remembered him looking healthy so it really helped me for him not to look like himself. It felt like he wasn't dead anymore. It felt like he was still here. Listening to the service, they were talking about his kids and how good his relationships were with them. They talked about how he was such a great and amazing person, then they referred to me as his step child. I looked around and actually stopped crying. They had me all kinds of fucked up. *They had no idea that I knew that information, so why the fuck would they say that shyt out loud or put it in the obituary? It's all good though watch me carry shyt.*

In came Big Neise, the woman they *thought* they banned. She walked down the aisle looking like she was hurt. She was pausing every couple of seconds, I don't think she was ready to see him go. Either that, or she couldn't believe it. Once she approached the casket she stared at him intently for a while. When I think she just needed a second to get herself together, Earnest walked over to her and told her to leave. I was hip at the time because it was only a couple of pews over from me. All I did was watch her leave; I figured maybe she was going to the bathroom.

I did get up to go find her, but by the time I got outside she was gone. I asked around to see what had happened but one of my cousins to me that she was asked to leave. I mean I heard they banned her but who actually does that shyt? That was his wife and the mother of his kids. Smh.

Watching them roll him down in the ground, his dumb ass family members, not all but some, had the audacity to throw this rinky dink ass funeral. How is this man a two time Vietnam Veteran, was in the United States Army and I didn't even see a pigeon, a bird, a dog, a frog... where the fuck was the tribute? The nigga didn't even have a plaque. I have never been to such a dumb ass, disrespectful funeral. Might as well had put my dad in a cardboard box, taped it up, wrote rest in peace in crayon and kicked that bitch in the hole and let some one's pit bull kick the dirt over it.

On top of that shyt, some random adult lady was there talking about she was his daughter... and they had the audacity to give her my dad's flag! That flag should have went to Graham because he was his only son!

At that point, I was done. I was completely over it. I had officially seen it all. I just didn't understand how this nigga did so much for them for them to turn around and treat him like that. I would never be able to find his ass at the cemetery.

A couple of weeks later things were rough. Everything just felt off. I couldn't believe that he wasn't there. All the laughs and arguments were gone. I used to actually look forward to the arguments between him and my mom because it was exciting and it was our normal. Crazy thing is that was once I accepted that, I was much better off. Things were a bit dry now – especially since I didn't have my backbone now. So, it was time for me to get me some money. I didn't have daddy to give me hundreds of dollars at a time on top of my own money anymore. I had gotten used to walking around with a certain amount of money too; it was my goal to get it myself since my help was gone. Before I knew it, I was working in Silver Spring at the Potbelly's and the Borders right across the street from each other. It was not only very convenient for me, but I was getting a lot of money only to be 18. The only thing was that I wasn't driving yet and my dad always told me he was going to get me a car. Yes, he passed first, but in due time, I had gotten one on my own. I had turned 18 in boot camp and that was cool, but I not only wanted to be grown, I wanted to be a parent. I lost another baby after the one in 2005 damn near the same day a year later. I basically just wanted to be in the best position I could be if that time came.

2008

Still working and doing my thing, everything was chill.
Things were going great surprisingly. Me and Oliver were
still doing us, so that was cool. Me and my mom really
didn't have many problems because I was staying with
Oliver. There were days where I was like *why the fuck am I
here?* He was still sweet and all that, and he still catered to
me, but he always had people around and he was always
on moves. He just couldn't sit still and it irritated me
sometimes but whatever. I was in my own little world there.

For my birthday that year, I just wanted to be happy and I
kinda was. I was contemplating going into the military, so I
was running around getting information for that in between
me going to work.

MAY 15TH

My birthday! I always treated my birthday like it was a holiday. I didn't really go out much but I would buy myself whatever. The night of my birthday, Oliver told me to come over and I did. For the first time, I was drinking and having a good time with him instead of chilling in the room and him being God knows where. This was the night of my life for some reason... sex that night was different, but I liked it a lot. He just always made a way for me to feel special.

Following my birthday, I really started to entertain the idea of the military. Military screamed stability, money, happiness, and it was just a ticket to travel the world, have peace of mind, and meet some great people. I spoke with a recruiter to try to get an idea of what I was getting myself into. Once I got some facts, my mind was made up and I was out of here. They set up an appointment to make sure that I was physically fit to participate in my duties to serve my wild ass country. I was told that I had to visit my doctor and one of their doctors.

That month flew by. I would have sworn to God that He was trying to get me out of here. I sat in the waiting room for what felt like hours. Seeing person after person getting up when I knew that I came in before them was beginning to irritate me. After sitting there for two hours, I began to gather my things to leave when magically, my name was called. Once I stood up for some reason I had this really nervous kind of feeling in my stomach like butterflies. I didn't know why. Each patient room I passed I felt like I was in a daze and I had the effects of a blind person except I could see. I heard the air hit my ears to let me know I passed through an open space. Everyone was moving very slowly and I guess I become incoherent because the nurse repeatedly calling my name but I never answered. Finally, she tapped me on my shoulder and instantly everything went back to normal. I was on Mississippi Ave by Southern Ave station at the Arc.

I looked at the nurse like I was out of it and said, "I'm sorry I didn't hear you."

"I see. Is everything okay?"

"Yes, I guess I just excited and a little nervous. I can't believe I'm actually thinking about going into the military."

 "Well that's good. What branch?"

"Army."

"That's good, congratulations! The doctor will be in shortly to begin you physical and to get some bloodwork."

As the nurse took her exit, I found a place to put my belongings. In my mind, I'm like super excited and super nervous about this move, but it was what needed to be done. At the same time, I was scared to fuckin die but too late for that shyt, right?

I climbed on the hospital bed that I would normally lay down on, but today I choose to sit up and look around. I really liked reading all of the posters on the wall while I waited. It always took my mind off of how long these people take to do their job. The doctor had finally arrived and it was a really nice looking lady. She was medium height, slim, had long nice hair with the best teeth I saw ever in life. Not to mention, she had a smile that could light up a room.

"Hello Nichole, how are you? I'm Dr. Lee I'm going to start with taking your blood so we can try to have your blood results as soon as possible. We don't want you waiting on a phone call."

I always hated getting my blood drawn. In my head I'm like, *shyt how the fuck can I get out of this because I always get dizzy and I always feel like I'm gonna pass out. It's just a lot getting my blood drawn. I got it. I'm going to just go to the bathroom lol.*

The doctor drew my blood and once again I was on the verge of passing out! My eyes got heavy and she laughed shook her head and said, "How do you have tattoos but can't get you blood drawn?"

"It's just not the same," I laughed, too.

She left out the room with tubes of my blood and I felt relieved that it was over. I felt relieved that blood results can be transferred from doctor to doctor because I wasn't doing this shyt again later – it takes too much out of me! The doctor put me through a series of tests, none of which I failed. The doc also took vitals and did an ear screening along with the vision test (which always proves I'm blind as shyt). During these observations, the nurse came in with the blood results and asked me to give a urine sample. Before I left out the room to head for the bathroom my doctor stopped me she said, "You're 6 weeks pregnant! Is this a good thing? Do you know who the father is? Do I need to explain your options?"

In my mind, I was so fucking siced and I was looking at her like *options? Bitch I'm keeping my damn baby!* I felt like this was my third pregnancy and I was determined not to miscarry... well... if I could help it. I didn't know how I was gonna tell Oliver but at the same time, something was telling me to get an abortion, which was quickly starting to become a better option. And that's what I intended to do. I was beginning to become fearful and regretful and I just wanted to leave.

I told the doctor I had to go and quickly left. I headed to the bus stop across the street that damn near was in the woods. I was so knocked off my game but I headed to Oliver's house to deliver the news. Not sure of how he was going to take it because he was already spreading that he had a baby on the way, so I was just annoyed. As I was walking up to the door, I just walked in, noticing that it was open. I asked where Oliver was located in the house and someone I didn't know pointed upstairs. He was in Wodie's room watching TV so I walked in. I sat there with him to ask him about his day and I told him about mine. He must have sensed something was wrong because he asked me, "What's wrong? What's on your mind?"

"I'm six weeks pregnant." Fear overcame me because I didn't know what he was going to say or how he was going to feel. I looked at him intently. I watched his facial expressions and body language, but I couldn't read anything... then he spoke.

"What are we going to do?"

"I'm going to get an abortion."

"Nah, we having a baby."

He seemed happy. I felt happy, I was relieved. I wasn't sure how this was going to work, but it was happening. I wasn't going to tell my mother, but I was officially having a baby. I was going to do whatever to make sure I made it to full term.

It felt like I was the happiest I had ever been. I loved Oliver and for the first time, I knew in my heart this baby was gonna make it. After my second miscarriage on September 1, 2006, I started feeling like I was having fertility issues. I started getting scared of being pregnant and started to not even entertain the thought of having a baby. If it was one thing in the world that I wanted to be when I grew up, I wanted to be a mother. A mother to a bunch of kids. I admired my mom for having four children. Even though she had her faults, she was a great mother. We never wanted for anything and all of our needs were met, now our wants were a different story.

Oliver and I seemed as if we were getting closer. He was beginning to make me accept him and rely on him. When I say accept him, I mean accept that he is about to become my child's father. I liked the thought of it; it was starting to make sense. Oliver was everything in terms of how he cared for me. He didn't put anyone before me – he fed me anytime I asked him. He was making sure I got to and from his house to my mom's house. I rarely ever went home but when I did it was always bullshyt.

On the rare occasion that I went home, me and Brittany got into it. Apparently, my mother told my sister that I took her money out of the drawers in her room. The thing was, I was just coming to swap clothes out so I could leave again. I had two jobs, so there was no reason for me to steal. Me and Brittany were close enough that I could have just asked her and nine out of ten times she would have given it to me. Every now and then I might take stuff from her like food, clothes, Halloween costumes and stuff but I didn't need to take her money. Brittany approached me and asked me "Why did you take my money? Give me my money back."

We of course started arguing because that shyt had blew me. That wasn't even the worse part; my mother was standing there instigating the whole thing. Not to mention she never saw me take a thing. Brittany and I started tousling and arguing. With no help from my mom, I felt like they were both coming at me. I ended up getting cut in my ear. My ear was bleeding like shyt and I was pissed. All of this was going on while I'm pregnant with my child. At the time, I didn't know what I was having. Everyone assumed that I was having a boy because of how I was carrying. My mother still didn't know and I was ok with that. My pregnancies were the one thing that my dad never found out about. One thing I could say about my mom was that she never told my secrets.

The pregnancy was really fun, but stressful for me. The fun part was that I got to feel my baby grow inside of me. Watching my body transform into this huge, yet shapely figure was crazy. My face was getting fatter, my butt was plump, and I went from a 32A to a 34B. My hair grew and was really pretty. Nothing bad had come from this pregnancy as far as my looks and build were concerned. I was glowing. I was surprised that my mom hadn't noticed because I was three months along. I was really big, but at the time, I carried small. You could still tell because of the way I carried and how my body transformed.

The stressful part was that I was constantly worrying about losing my baby. I would make myself pee just to see if there was any blood. I told myself once I hit four months then I would relax. I didn't have far to go but boy was I anxious. Every cramp, pain, ache you name it I was in the emergency room. I did not play. One day I literally was in pain in the pit of my stomach and I ran to the ER. I called Oliver and just like I thought, he was there. He came with every friend he had. During this time, they gave me my emergency sonogram and accidentally mentioned my son. So, I finally knew what I was having. I was having a boy. I was mad and I cried about it. I wanted a girl so badly. It took me a while to adjust to the fact that I was having a boy. I had started to get boy things to make myself feel better. I brought something almost every day. I was totally obsessed with buying baby things and don't let me get started about the baby channel. Watching that shyt everyday had me wanting to have my baby right then and there. They had me buying even more stuff after I would see how they decorated the baby rooms.

I was curious to know what it looked like to have a baby. Like what were they going through, what the vagina look like when the head comes out? Only because I wouldn't get that perspective I would only know the feeling of having a baby. I had all my routine appointments and they went great... just hearing my baby's heart beat amazed me. It made my heart melt. I knew that as soon as I saw him, I would fall in love completely. Seeing his little feet and tiny hands and beautiful eyes would be worth it all.

I went to go talk to Oliver about the baby and make him aware of my findings. He had left before I got my sonogram, so he did not know that we were having boy. I knew he was gonna be pressed because I think he wanted a boy.

Approaching Oliver's door I heard a lot of laughter and just a lot of people. I twisted the knob to walked in and instantly started look for him. I went in his room to drop my things off and he was in there on the bed. I sat down beside him we hugged and fell back on the bed. I asked him was he ready for his son.

He just stared at me for a second and touched my stomach and repeated, "A boy?"

We talked about baby names and we just had casual conversation. One topic in particular came up. Oliver had mentioned to me that he didn't know what he wanted to get into and he really didn't know where his life was going. So, I mentioned and suggested he go into the military because that insures stability, money, and a way out of Kenilworth. We talked about a number of different things and I gave him all the answers to what he wanted to know. We ended the conversation with me letting him know that I knew a recruiter he could talk to who could explain the signing bonus and everything else. As far as I knew, I was getting him on the right track and Oliver was going into the Army Reserves. That way, our kid could be straight and Oliver would be good. I had me, so I never worried about me.

* * *

I was finally five months pregnant and pressed because as long as my son was still kicking, I was having a baby. However, I wasn't always happy. Out of nowhere, me and Oliver took a turn for the worst. It was like he just switched up on me. He just started treating me like shyt. I was bitches and shyt to him now. I couldn't for the life of me understand it; like what the fuck did I do to him?

I was on my way home from work – I worked at the IHOP out Forestville. I was living with Oliver officially now, I had a key and everything. I got there and to my surprise no one was there, not even Oliver. I went in the room, it was dark outside and this nigga had this lil ass light in his room that didn't light up shyt. I noticed a big black trash bag in the middle of the room in front of the closet. My heart dropped and something kept telling me to look in the bag. I saw my shyt in the bag, so I instantly got frustrated because if he wanted me to leave I would have. I wasn't homeless, he asked to be here. So instead of just leaving in a cab because that was my first thought, I decided to wait until he got there and everybody else too because I swear he was always faking about everything. I wanted him to see me leave and not have one problem with it. Shyt, I figured if I just left while he was gone it would have made me look mad. Then he did all that for nothing because he was gonna stop me. I was sure of it. I was waiting for like two hours. Oliver and the gang came back. It wasn't everybody though – just the people that stayed in the house.

He walked around me ignoring me and acting like I wasn't there, I guess he was blown because he didn't have anyone to fake for – just his family who knew better. After so much acting like I wasn't there, I simply called a cab and he heard me do so. While he was ignoring me, he sat out there in the living room. I stayed in the room. I didn't even bother trying to work things out with him.

Waiting damn near forty-five minutes, my cab finally pulls up. I grabbed all my things and headed towards the door. As I was leaving, he was in the perfect spot to see me because he was on the long couch against the wall of his room.

In my mind, I'm literally trying to figure how long he gonna play this game. I don't know who the fuck he was around when he did that pointless shyt but they weren't there for him to see him earn his academy award. I had one foot in the cab when I got a yank on my arm. I said, "What are you doing?"

"Aye my man, you can go. She don't need no cab." This is what he said to the cab driver. The driver looked at me for the final confirmation for him to leave. I paid him no mind and asked Oliver, "Why did you even put my shyt in the bag in the first place?"

"I heard that you was talking to some other nigga. So, I said you out there, let me just let you be."

"What? Out there? What are you talking about? Nigga I be with you."

He carried my stuff back in the house and we watched TV and talked about the events that had been going on between us. We also talked about the fact that he was getting ready to go away for the military.

For some reason things were starting to just take a turn for the worst. Me and Oliver weren't me and Oliver anymore. He was a different person. It was like he didn't respect me as his child's mother or as the girl he'd been kicking it with forever. I guess he had a lot going on; he had another baby on the way, and she was four months ahead of me. Oliver was set to leave and it was bothering me a little bit because I felt like I was going to be alone.

The day he did leave, it was just me and him there, to my surprise. The blower was that I had to go back to my mother's house for her to get on my damn nerves. I said my goodbyes and he actually looked like he was sad to be leaving me. It was the one day that he didn't act funny... he actually held me close. He told me he would write me every week. I just hoped the time apart was gonna bring us closer. Honestly, I was more like forget us, I just wanted him to be a great dad but only time would tell.

* * *

Being back at home, things were okay for the time being. I felt as though eventually my mother would act crazy. She was aware that I was having a baby, and of course she was cold about it. She really didn't have a response which was fine with me. I honestly just wanted to be left alone. The one person that I missed was Brittany; I missed having a friend, doing stuff with her, and going out. I also didn't talk to my sister much, so I was happy to see her.

I was definitely ready to drop my baby once I hit six or seven months. He was in my ribs the entire time and I hated it because it hurt. The baby was also making me sick. I was sick my whole second trimester. I was also sick and tired of the anticipation of this pregnancy. The more I watched Labor and Delivery, the more I was trying to make my baby come. Now what I *was* enjoying was this body. I felt like the prettiest girl in the world and apparently so did the boys. It was like they didn't care that I was pregnant. Everyone was still trying to talk to me. I mean EVERYONE – including Double A.

He was probably the closest thing to a boyfriend I had, except he wasn't my boyfriend. The sexual attraction was crazy. I already knew damn well I wasn't gonna touch him sexually because I was pregnant. But he was great at keeping my attention. He came over a couple of times and chilled, but that was the most attractive thing about him. He chilled. He didn't pressure me. He wasn't disrespectful. He was just himself, and he was cute as hell doing it. Brittany was talking to one of his men which made it convenient. I never really wanted to be by myself with him anyway.

I normally would check the mail every Friday to see if Oliver wrote me. What was crazy was I thought he wasn't gonna write me. I really wasn't sure why, but every time I received a letter I was surprised. In some of the letters he sent me, he wrote some of the sweetest things and he also made phone calls, too. It really used to make my day because I really did miss him and I wish I could have seen him. But… he had to do what he had to do. He wanted me to send him pics so he could track the process of my pregnancy. I went out and brought a camera just to take pics and send them to him.

Going into my eighth month, Oliver was able to come home and visit. Words couldn't express how much I needed to see him – I was lonely and I was spoiled and I wanted to be under him. Even though he wasn't here for long, you know I came running to him. We were getting ready for the holidays, which was my favorite time of year, because I was big on family.

Thanksgiving was the upcoming holiday and a fat girl's dream. I was ready to eat anything and everything, my mother was cooking so I knew that I was going to eat whatever she baked, broiled, fried, and/or grilled. Though Oliver couldn't be there, he called and made the day better. I also had a good time with my mother and sister.

Christmas and New Years came and went. Before I knew it, January was the final month of the pregnancy and I was exhausted. I was so over being pregnant and it was crazy because I was having labor pains every day, all day. I was as big as a house and eating everything in sight. I was so in tune with my baby and I couldn't wait to meet him. I had everything I needed for him thanks to me and his Godmother. The downside was I was sick to death of being in the house. My best friend Dimples was going out and I insisted on going because honestly all I wanted to do was listen to music, and that was it. I never went out or did anything while I was pregnant, and it wasn't against the law to have fun. We were set to go out January 24th which was a Saturday, and my due date was January 29th. So this was my bang, and yea I knew that I was pushing it but he wasn't due yet so all was fair.

I felt really pretty pregnant, so I was just trying to hang out. I was seriously tired of being alone and crying. This pregnancy was really emotional for me. All I ate was chicken and french fries, so I actually wanted to smell something different. We got to the club and of course the bouncer was looking at me like I was crazy.

What blew mine was that in my mind, I felt as though it was nothing wrong with being pregnant and going out and having a good time. Now, I understand the risk, but it ain't that deep. I wasn't out here bullshyting around fighting and all into shyt. I was just a pregnant girl who was tired of sitting around.

So now we were in the building and everything was everything. The sound of the music made my night and I was happy for the first time in a minute. Well happy that I was out and chilling instead of in the house eating. I received a phone call from my son's father, so I ran outside to hear. "Hello?"

"Aye man, where the fuck you at?"

I lied. I don't really know why I lied, but I did. My heart dropped and I felt like I was in trouble. I just wanted to get the hell off the phone. I just didn't want to hear that shyt. I was ready to go home. In my mind, I knew it was about to be some shyt. But on the bright side, not today cause his ass was gone. "I'm running around with Dimples... but I'm gonna call you when I get back to her house."

"Yea, aight."

I was ready to go home at that point. I had no interest in being out anymore. I just had a bad feeling. I couldn't put my finger on it, but I went back in and I tried to have a good night. Well, what was left of it.

As the night ended, I was cramping something serious. I knew it wasn't the real thing though. What was crazy is that six and a half months earlier, he was already trying to come out. I was two centimeters and they had to give me a shot to stop my contractions. He wasn't playing no games at all – he wanted to meet his momma. As we pulled back up at Dimples' house, I just wanted to lay down; instead, I received a phone call from Oliver. As soon as I answered he asked, "Where the fuck you at?"

"I'm at Dimples house, why?"

"Where the hell is that at?"

"Around W Street. She lives on W Street."

"I'm on my way."

"Okay."

But wait… when in the fuck did he even come home?! And what made him want to come get me? I guess I'll see once he pulls up. I just remember looking at Dimples and feeling sick to my stomach. My stomach was cramping and it was blowing me that I really didn't know what to expect from Oliver. I was getting too stressed.

I barely even let my phone ring before I answered, "Hello?"

"Come outside, man."

"What color car are you in and what are you driving?"

"Black truck."

"Okay." I hung up and went outside, but in my head my heart was in my ass. I instantly lost my appetite. I felt like I was going to pass out.

Of course, once I opened the door, I realized I'd be in a car full of niggas – drunk niggas at that. Oliver really didn't say much at the time. It was pretty much a very quiet ride home. The closer to Kenilworth we got, the sleepier and sleepier I got. I didn't want to stay up, I simply wanted the day to be over. Pulling up to the house, I quickly jumped out the truck and tried to be the first one at the door. As soon as we stepped foot into the room, the disrespect started. I was all kinds of bitches and dumb asses all over again. He even went that hard in front of people. My feelings were hurt and at that point I wanted to go home. Everything that he was doing in that moment was uncalled for... questioning me, asking me if that was his son and all of that. All I could do was look at him.

Was I shocked? No, not quite.

Was I amazed? Hell yea, because I had never met a more disrespectful nigga in my life. I shook my head, turned over, and went to sleep.

The following morning, I woke up ready to go. When I sat up, Oliver wasn't there... well, he wasn't in the room. I was just about to get up when I noticed the door knob turning. Oliver walked into the room and Ace was behind him. Oliver stopped and looked at me and asked Ace, "Ain't this bitch dumb?" Ace stood there surprised and simply said, "Aye go head, Oliver." He left the room and shut the door.

Oliver walked over to me, sat beside me, and started trying to have sex with me.

I was lying there like *is this nigga crazy? He was just in here showing off like shyt. All to turn around and try to have sex with this stupid dumb bitch. I don't even know what the fuck he mad at, I mean shyt you would have thought I fucked another nigga or something. I think that this nigga be putting on shows for whoever the hell around. Smdh.* Oliver was the type that always did too much and then he wanted to smooth things over after. In my mind, I was just sitting there like *wateva let's just do this shyt.* Having sex was an easy way to have my baby and start my contractions. Especially because I didn't walk a lot. I was fat.

He started sliding my underwear off and playing with my vagina. He was talking to me, which always turned me on. Oliver was just a piece of work. He got on top of me and as soon as he entered me, my whole body felt relaxed. He was sort of rough, to my surprise. He never handled me a certain way. He was always sweet and caring, loving, attentive, affectionate, a real Nichole pleaser. Not today though. He was trying to hurt me in a reasonable kind of way. The deeper he went, and he was blessed, the more I started to feel pain. The more he moaned the more stimulated I became. When I felt this particular pain, I knew he was coming. I screamed, "STOP OLIVER!"

"I'm not stopping nothing." He moved my hands out of the way. The pain was so intense, I mean like real intense, I started to tear up. So I said again, "Oliver... stop please, it hurts!" He would not stop. I really don't know if he believed me or what, but I swear I wasn't lying. It got to the point where I started banging on his chest and screaming. He stopped, looked at me, and asked me, "Are you okay?"

"No! NO! NO! NO! NO! It hurts really bad I need to go to the hospital!" Oliver was so excited, he even tried to count the contractions and he didn't even know what the hell he was doing. He had to go back to the military that day, so I assumed he wasn't gonna be there next to me when I had our baby.

On one hand, I understood that he had to go back to work. But on another hand, this was considered an emergency and I was sure they would have given him leave. For the first time, I think I realized that he didn't give a fuck about me or my son, which was cool because the moment I had my baby he had one year to get it right. Just one. If he did not, we were done. I put that on my father because I was never interested in being a baby momma or having baby daddy drama. Hell, I didn't even want the baby daddy. Just the kid if I'm keeping it real. So, if he wanted to be a fuck up that would be on him, not me. Only time would tell and I knew that I sure as hell would see.

I asked if he could take me to the hospital and he told me he couldn't. I rolled my eyes so hard because I was in pain I was hurting. I never felt a pain like this before. I don't know how many baby shows I watched to try to prepare for this, but NOTHING prepared me for this. Nothing could help me understand why this shyt hurt so bad. One thing about me was that I was ready. I wanted to see him. I swore that I was gonna be the best mother I could be.

* * *

I called my mother because Oliver couldn't do it and there was no one else in the house to take me. My mother told me she had company and that she wasn't gonna stop what she was doing to take me to the hospital. I held the phone shaking my head. I couldn't believe that she just told me she had company. So from that point on, I felt like I was alone. I couldn't even get to the hospital. Luckily, I heard the front door open and it was Oliver's sister. He asked her to take me and she agreed. I quickly jumped in the car. Even though I would've liked to go to Georgetown, she ended up taking me to PG Hospital because it was closer.

I was in her front seat kicking on the dashboard crying and slouched down as far as I could go in the seat. I couldn't believe this shyt was happening. It was January 25, 2009 at like three in the afternoon. And it was set to snow. It wasn't cold, but you can smell the snow coming. The air was clean and crisp. It calmed me a little bit as we walked from the car to the ER doors. I could barely walk, so a nurse rushed out to sit me in a wheel chair. I called my sister because she was truly my best friend. Brittany would do anything for me. I loved that about her; it's been that way since childhood. When she answered, I told her, "Britt I'm in labor! I'm having the baby... I'm at PG Hospital."

"Damn! I was just up there!" She said to her boyfriend, "Aight Kolby, turn around. Nichole having her baby! She up PG." Brittany was there damn near before I got upstairs to the labor and delivery ward.

Once I was given a room, my water still hadn't broke and the doctor told me that I was only two centimeters still and they will probably be letting me go soon. I was there for almost two hours. I texted my brother Wannell to tell him I was in labor and he texted me back basically telling me to take it easy and I got this.

Wannell was my admiration. Growing up, little did he know he was my idol. I always looked up to him. I wanted to do everything just like him. I wanted to be just like him. I got on his nerves just to get attention from him and I kinda used to be bad so my parents wouldn't think I could handle being home alone and he would have to watch me. He was just a big brother and my soul purpose in life was to irritate him!

The only sibling I didn't talk to was my brother Graham. I never really knew how to get in touch with him. Graham was the type to do his own thing. He liked to be out the way – a quiet, smart nigga. He moved in silence. I knew that once my brother caught wind that I was having my baby, he would be there. He was big on family and I think he liked kids but just didn't want to admit to it.

The doctor ended up discharging me because they felt like the baby wasn't coming. I was so blown. I just said fuck it whatever; all I wanted to do was have my damn son and I just started to cry. I'm not sure where my sister went, but I didn't care. I simply took the long way in the building and I walked and used the steps. As I was walking down this extremely long hall way, I was starting to regret walking should have just got my fat ass on the elevator like the White people would have done. I picked up the phone and called my grandma to see if she could get Mr. Davis to come and get me to take me back home. She told me that she would call him and see, but when I got downstairs he was already there. So was my sister.

When I got in Mr. Davis car, I wasn't in the car for forty-five seconds and half way down the parking lot before my water broke. I looked down at my watch it was 5:46 pm. It was warm and a lot of fluids. I had to apologize for my son being disrespectful and trying to come into the world in his car before I got out. The nurse came out to wheel chair me back to labor and delivery and she asked me who did I want in the room with me.

I couldn't answer because I was in too much pain. My aunt Nette said she will go.

The look on Brittany's face was the blower. She wanted to be in the room, and I wanted her to be there, too. I was just in too much pain. I mean, I can understand where she was coming from and how she felt but it wasn't intentional at all I was just in pain.

In the delivery room tired out my mind and just needing a damn break, I was ready for it to be over with already. I literally wasn't ready for none of this. I got into the hospital bed and put my feet up in the stirrups and I was getting ready to push. The nurse was telling me all the rules of pushing, when to push, how to push, etc. All I knew was that I had to take a shyt so I jumped up to head to the bathroom when the nurse stopped me and said, "What are you about to do?"

"I have to use the bathroom, I gotta take a number two. I'm thirsty and I need some food."

"Oh my gosh, no! Let's go, you're ready now and you don't have to poop, your baby is coming!" I climbed back in the bed pissed because I was hungry and I really wanted to eat but hey whatever.

"Okay sweetie, I'm going to tell you when to push okay?"

"It hurts, it hurts, it hurts! I want drugs! Give me some drugs or something now!"

"You're doing great hun, you just had a contraction and they are very close now so it's just about that time to push. Okay? Push Nichole!"

"OMG I can't! I can't breathe and its hurts." At that point, I was crying hysterically and hyperventilating. I never felt pain like that in my life.

"It's happening sweetheart, the baby is coming! I can see his head. Just keep pushing okay? Ready Nichole? And GO!"

"I'm tired... I'm... Stop... I can't. I need drugs! I want the epidural!" And before you know it, at 6:46 pm my baby boy entered the world. 6 pounds 2 oz. I hadn't looked at him yet because I was completely exhausted.

"Can I see my son?"

"Your son? You have a daughter."

I wanted a girl so bad! I literally cried when they told me I was having a boy. I mean I was happy to have a baby, but I really, really wanted a girl. Now that I had a girl, I didn't even know how to feel. I was just so overjoyed with tears. Like I couldn't even touch her. The nurse tried to bring her over to me but I pushed back. I really could not touch her. She had no clue how bad I wanted her. She also didn't have a clue about how much I was going to love her. She wasn't gonna want for anything. It was love and I hadn't even touched her.

I was crying for what seemed like hours. By the time I was ready to hold her, it was after her first bath and I was all settled into my room. The nurse brought me my baby girl and I laid there pinching myself like I could not believe or wrap my mind around having a baby. My mind started to drift off while I was holding her. I was wondering how it would have been with my mom and her dad right here... but, of course, they weren't. Oliver just didn't care to be here and my mother didn't bother to show up. Cool. But guess who I did have? Brittany. She told me she was gonna stay with me while I was in the hospital. Honestly, I was surprised because it was hard prying her away from her boyfriend. I definitely appreciated it though.

My Brother came and that moved heaven and earth for me. Wannell didn't really show up for nothing or anyone, but he always showed up for me when it counted. I never would have thought he would have come. That's the big Navy man with lots of other shyt to do. He held her and chilled with us for a second, and then he left. Another thing that was surprising was that it was snowing and had snowed heavily enough for him to stay home, and yet, he still managed to come up. That was the highlight besides having my sister there helping me and keeping me company.

The next day passed and I had to get down to the bottom of what I was gonna name her. I never really thought about it because I was still tripped out about me having a little girl. A little me. I thought about naming her something similar to her father but but fuck no. I had a bad feeling about him. I don't know if it was because he started off wrong, but he only had one year to prove himself. If not, like I said before, I would be gone. At this point, it was all about my daughter and if he wouldn't be around, it would be his loss. I decided to name her Masiah. I let Graham and Brittany give her a middle name to bond with her; that way when the baby asks where she got her names from, there would be a story behind it. Graham gave her the middle name Zyair and Brittany gave her the middle name Cori just like Jay-Z. (We were crazy about that man and Beyoncé.) I named her Masiah to give her more of an advantage in a male dominated world. I figured that employers will take more of a chance thinking that she is a male than to take a chance on a bomb female with a banging resume.

I called James several times to see if he was coming to the hospital got and no answer. What surprised me was that I felt like I wanted him there. I felt like he should have been there. I found it crazy that he didn't want to see, meet, or hold his daughter for the first time. I guess it was because it wasn't his first daughter. His first daughter was born four months before Masiah on the same day, which made them exactly four months apart. It was okay though, because seeing my baby girl was fascinating. I never knew love until I laid eyes on her. She had the brightest eyes and she was a good baby. She was mine!

The next day came and I was still pinching myself, still in amazement. I was completely lost looking at her. I swore she was the best thing that ever happened to me. I was still in awe with her beauty, her skin, her little feet, her curly, thin hair. She had developed my features, but she had her daddy's face.

She slept really long, though I felt myself waking her up so I could see her with her eyes open. I had protective issues when it came to her. I would watch her intently to make sure she was breathing... meaning I would watch her stomach move and put my finger under her nose. She was that serious for me. If I had lost my baby, I don't know what I would've done. People always asked me to hold my baby. I would quickly say, "Nah, I'm good." I just couldn't chance it. That went for my mother as well. I just didn't know about my mother and my daughter being too close because I never wanted to do something I regretted.

Once I finally went back home, I was pressed that I got to be in the comfort of my own home. I really wasn't dealing with my mom because of how she carried it when I went into labor. Brittany was a big help, plus I think that she thought Masiah was kinda cool. For me, I had to get used to being a mother... meaning taking her everywhere I went. My daughter slept through the night, so I didn't have to wake up in the middle of the night or anything like that. Masiah was easy. I knew what she was like from the start – she loved to listen to the vacuum and water run, then I'd give her a warm bottle, and a good pat on the ass and she was gone for the night. Then when she woke up she loved to just stare at the ceiling while she played with her hands.

Masiah was showing early signs of being advanced. She was holding her bottle and trying to scoot, putting her own pacifier in her mouth and everything. I could tell she was comfortable with herself and that she didn't bother anyone because she wasn't needy at all.

One morning for some reason I slept hard and slept till like noon. I never used to put Masiah in her bed because I always wanted her next to me. I made her sleep on my chest. Once I woke up I noticed my baby wasn't there. It was a weekday so I thought I was the only one home because my sister was in school and my mom had to work. The state department didn't play with her. My heart dropped and I started to panic. I jumped up searched the house. I looked everywhere but my mother's room because she would always lock her door and I didn't have the key. Tears streamed down my face and I started going off. My mother opened her door trying to figure out what was going on. I kept screaming, "Where is my baby?" and my mother replied, "Girl you need to calm the hell down Masiah is fine, she woke up and you was still sleep so I took her, washed her up, and fed her. She wasn't crying or anything but you was sleep so..."

I grabbed my baby and was furious. "Ma don't just take my baby and lock her in the room with you." I was always scared because my mother had a real bad drinking habit and I didn't want any mistakes with my kid – none. We went into the room and I instantly started to feel bad because I didn't mean to hurt her feelings, but that kind of shyt was scary to me. As I was sitting there thinking about whether to apologize to my mom, my phone started to ring. I never did rush to my phone because most of the time it was no one I wanted to talk to. Whoever this was really wanted me to answer but I got there too late. They let the phone ring until the voicemail picked up. Getting closer to the phone, it stopped ringing. I looked at the missed call and, surprise, surprise. It was Oliver.

Before I called back, I thought to myself. *It took three days to call and see what's up with his daughter.* I couldn't help but think what the hell I got myself into to. I found it crazy because I felt like he wanted me to be crazy and wilding out about him like these other girls. No. Not I. I was different. I wasn't the pressed type, I wasn't one of them girls who needed to do all that. I didn't need him or anyone else. I had me and Si and that was all that mattered. I really didn't have time to play with this nigga at all. But once again, in a year we'd see because I was not playing with him. If it came down to it, we would be gone, no exceptions, as of January 25th, 2010.

I called him back and off bucks he answered with a question "What the fuck you doing?"

"Taking care of my baby. Why what's up?"

"I'm about to come through there."

"Well, okay. When are you coming?"

"I'll be there."

I hung up the phone because, for some reason, Oliver was starting to get on my bad side. He wasn't someone I knew anymore. I was quickly growing tired but I wasn't done. I just wanted him to step up to the plate and take care of his responsibilities as a man. Maybe he would, maybe he wouldn't. No matter what he did, I had to do what I had to do.

Hours later I heard a knock at the door. Once I got out into the living room, before I even got to the door, I shook my head. This nigga couldn't even come see his kid by himself. He had to bring a bunch of niggas with him like he was going to a damn concert or some shyt. That irritated me real bad. I just didn't see the point of that. I would have at least thought he would have come alone to bond with her. Clearly, I was wrong. He only came just so no one could say that he didn't. He looked at her and said she looks like you as if she didn't look just like his ass. I didn't respond. He said what he said, then he left with his men.

With plenty of time to think to myself and get my thoughts together, I quickly came to the conclusion that he wasn't gonna do right. This wouldn't end how I expected it to, nor how I wanted it to, but alright. The games began and the gloves came all the way off.

* * *

Watching my baby grow was nothing short of exciting. Six months went past and Masiah was so fat and chunky. She appeared to fit in with the big kids. She was crawling and trying to talk. Her trying to talk would trip me out because she would really think she's holding an entire conversation. She would eat me out of house and home too, she loved adult food. I started making preparations for her birthday party because it was her first so it had to be big. I was finally getting the hang of things, so being a mother became second nature to me.

My friend Me Me had invited me to chill at the hotel with her and her boyfriend out Lanham – right there by the McDonalds on 450. This night I had maybe 2 drinks and I had my daughter so I wasn't really gonna do too much. Me Me called her father to come and get me and Si. Of course he came, but he wasn't happy. I was trying to understand what the hell he had an attitude for, but my baby was taken care of. Masiah was washed, fed, changed, and had actually fallen asleep.

When we got to his house, I would've been crazy if I thought he was alone. Even when he came to pick me up, he had a bunch of niggas with him. Why? I don't know. In his house there was nothing different. Oliver started hooping and hollering about me being there for another nigga and I'm just sitting here looking crazy because there wasn't even another dude present. Next thing you know, his hands went around my neck and he started to choke me. Oliver choked me until I stopped breathing. I woke up to him doing CPR. I woke up not knowing what was going on. The look on his face was fear. I guess he thought that I was gone. One of the first things I did was look for my baby but she was in his room sleep. I could tell that he felt bad, but I don't think he cared much. I went home shortly after and of course I took my baby because he was trying to holla, "I'm keeping my daughter!"

Boy please, yea right. The way I saw it was that he knew damn well he didn't do shyt for my baby. I was way past being nice or even paying his ass any attention. I really hoped that I wasn't pregnant again because I was done. I was still gonna give him the rest of the time needed to step up, but after that? Nah.

Me and my mother had a fallout again, and I was over that shyt too. In and out with my child. The back and forth… I really didn't feel like it was suitable for a baby so I decided to call one of my Godmothers to come and stay until I found my place. That's exactly what I did and I moved in on my Godsister's birthday in June.

This reminded me of a time again when I got fed up and I went to my Godsister Manda's house. Her mother treated me just like her own. What I loved the most about this situation was that Yo Yo was married and it reminded me of how I grew up before things got bad and my mother left. Yo Yo punished me just like a real kid and I honestly felt like I had another sister. Me and Manda argued like sisters but we were always back like we never left. She protected me in some ways and I liked that a lot. We used to sneak out and sneak back in. Things was crazy because we didn't get caught, but this is how I wished me and Brittany would have grown up. You know… just doing shyt that normal kids do. Not trying to live and survive as if we didn't have parents. Don't get me wrong, my mother did what was needed, but she kind of dropped the ball in a lot of areas. Yo Yo was hip to my mom because of Manda so there wasn't really many questions asked. She just opened her arms and her doors and she's been my Godmother ever since.

I was laying on the couch at Lisa's house and felt so sick I ran to the bathroom to go throw up. It caught me off guard because I stopped thinking I was pregnant when I started spotting. But me throwing up – and I never throw up – I kinda already knew what was up. I went to the store and got a pregnancy test.

I sat on the toilet in the bathroom trying to pee but I couldn't because I was anxious and I really didn't want to know nor did I want to be pregnant. Finally, I was able to pee with the assistance of the running water from the sink. I sat the test on the counter with the intentions of forgetting because if the test was positive, I was for sure getting an abortion. It would have been my first, but it wouldn't be my last if things wasn't right. And wasn't shyt right about this situation with me and Oliver. I went into the bathroom after my show went off to check the test and sure enough, I was pregnant. I was upset and blown about it because I had to get an abortion.

I called him up and told him I wanted to talk to him and he came. At the time, he had a girlfriend. I didn't really give two fucks about that because that didn't have anything to do with me and my daughter. He came and I was sitting in the car talking when another car pulled up and a girl hops out. Sure enough, it was his girlfriend. I just smiled and waved because what the fuck was she trying to do? That nigga wasn't about to let her get to me so it was no point in me or her getting hype because wasn't shyt about to happen. Oliver put his hands on her neck and he put her in the car. Oliver then got back in the car with me to finish our convo. I told him that I was gonna come to his house so he could take me to the abortion clinic and I wasn't leaving until he did. He was acting like he didn't want me to do it but that shyt was already happening and I didn't even make it there yet.

The abortion was scheduled for the next morning. He took me, but on the way home we got into a real bad argument. So bad that he spit in my face. My baby was in the back seat and so was his cousin. That was disrespectful on so many levels, so I immediately started kicking and punching. I was able to pull that off because I turned my back and laid against the door. I kicked and punched while he was driving until we pulled up at my house. Then, I kicked the door off of the hinges and tried to drive the car into a tree but he got to me first. We fought in the street for a second where he ripped my shirt and bra off then passed me and old sweater to put on so I can walk myself in the house.

Oliver sat my baby on the porch got back in his car and drove off.

This was what appeared to be one of the worst days of my life. I couldn't imagine ever being this disrespected and I was pissed. I was tired and most of all done dealing with his bullshyt. I literally wished that this nigga disappeared. I no longer was sending my daughter over there. I was just gonna focus on her and move the hell on.

By now, Masiah's first birthday had arrived and I couldn't be more excited. I never had any birthday parties, so I wanted her to have a big party. My mother was so pressed over my daughter, so of course she was there. My sister was in attendance, a few friends. One guest in particular was present and I didn't know how to feel. Oliver's other daughter's mother had brought Masiah's sister. Jay was cute as a button and a red bone just like her mother.

The party was going great; Masiah had a field day. My baby received any and everything from me. The cake was a double layered, princess kind. All I knew was that she was good and tired by the time that everyone had left. There was more than enough trash to clean up.

I ended up moving out of my Godmothers house due to a misunderstanding, then I moved in with Tish. Tish was easily one of the most important people in my life. Tish did the one thing that no one including my mother had done. She kept everything one hundred she explained to me that I couldn't stay there long because I needed to get out on my own. At the same time, she didn't mind me being there. She understood what I was going through, but didn't care enough to be my crutch. I was with her for a few months. It was one of the best things that happened to me.

Tish threw cabarets as her second job. She was about 5'6 and had a cute shape. She was successful in her own right. She had multiple jobs and a woman of many hats. I came in contact with Tish thru Shay. (Shay was another good friend of mine.) My kids and Shay's kids were cousins. Tish didn't have kids, so she was living her best life and I for one couldn't blame her.

It was February 27, 2010 and as soon as I got off work, I needed to find something to wear for this cabaret. I found a babysitter ASAP because that was the hardest part. I dropped Si off and headed home to get dressed.

We pulled up on the scene and the party was extremely dry at first but as the people started to arrive shyt starting getting turnt. Tish had to be there early because she threw these parties and at the time I was 20. All of her functions had to be 21 and over so I was parting with the heavy hitters. It was about 11:45 and I noticed this guy who was wearing black and purple. He had two of his mans with him and Swag and Surf was blasting from the speakers. They were dancing and having a good time. He had on dark purple foams, dark blue jeans, a black and purple graphic tee on with a black and purple hat with that big ass Jesus piece. What was so crazy was that it was endless, and when I say endless, I mean ENDLESS, niggas in this party. Old niggas, young niggas, light skin, dark skin, you name it. Of all the niggas there, I was only focusing on that one guy. I didn't know him, but I knew that I wanted to get to know him.

Unfortunately I was being followed and harassed by guys I wasn't even interested in, so I couldn't approach him. To top it off, I was pulled on stage by one of the band members. Shay walked off close to me and I grabbed her and told her to get his number for me. From onstage, I danced on one guy and was staring at another. To my surprise he was staring at me back. I took that as a good thing because I just knew that he was gonna be turned off. I mean why not? Why would anyone want a person that no-one else wants, right?

Eventually I managed to get close to him and he pulled me. I danced with him for what seemed like forever. I swear it seemed like love at first sight to me. I knew right then and there that I was gonna see what was up with the dude, but I didn't even know his name.

The night was almost over and he had asked me to take a picture with him. As soon as he asked me, the lights came on and then I quickly asked, "What's your name?" He looked back after slightly walking off and said "Rexx." I smiled, turned around, and walked off. The feeling that was in my stomach resembled butterflies and for the first time in a long I was interested, curious, nervous, and excited.

And I was here for it.

Tish and I were almost home when I decided to text him.

I knew it seemed thirsty, but what the hell?! I had to! I was crazy about a guy that I didn't know. I couldn't get him out of my head lol. When I saw him, it was like a movie. Everything was in slow motion, everyone around him were shadows, and the spotlight was on him. And Rexx was just my type too; he was 5'8, he was thick, light brown, and fresh as hell. He looked in between Plies and Chris Brown.

He had this mysterious thing about him that made me want to know more. He was calm in the club, he was attentive and alert. Rexx also wasn't intimidated by the other guys that was chasing me. So, I texted him and said:

Me 3:30am
Aye boy

Rexx 3:31am
Who dis?

Me 3:31am
Nichole

Rexx 3:33am
Wassup, you tryna come out?

Me 3:40am
I can. I mean are you gonna come to me because my baby in here sleep.

Rexx 3:41am
Yea I can text me the address and I'll be on my way.

I texted him my address and quickly got myself together. I put a bottle and a pacifier next to her. I slipped on some sweats and waited for him to tell me he was outside. I paced back and forth, knowing I was dead ass wrong for taking my ass outside and I had to go to work in a few hours. I was wondering if this nigga had a job because he was heading to me so late in the morning. I was gonna find out though. I was so nervous I didn't expect to see him this soon, but I was happy. There was just was something about this man. Then my phone went off.

Rexx 4:15am
   Here

I could have started sweating, I was so damn nervous. So nervous that I told Tish to give me an excuse not to go. She told me, "Girl take your ass outside. What? You rather it be Oliver?"

I looked at her with a frown on my face as I went out front to talk to the guy that I knew would soon be a problem, considering he had this effect on me in a matter of hours.

I walked to the door, popped a piece of gum in my mouth, and walked outside. I didn't know what car he was driving, but I saw him flash the lights. Before I walked over there I took a deep breath. I really hoped he wasn't a creep.

His car was hella nice. He drove a Buick that was baby blue and in the inside, it was clean as hell. On God, this man smelled heavenly. I wonder why I didn't smell him at the club. As soon as he laid eyes on me he smiled. He had a smile that would brighten up a room. The feelings I got were warm. I wanted him and from that point on my mission was to get him.

We talked about a number of different things; of course, I asked if he was unavailable because I wasn't really into guys with girls. It was funny because I figured he had a girl, but to my surprise he didn't. He said he was talking to a girl but that shyt was over a long time ago. I asked him what was he looking for and he felt like it would be nice to find a good girl he could vibe with, someone he could put a ring on. What was crazy is that I never thought about marriage until he said that. I mean... what would this mean? So I started trying to find out more about him, his background, some personal information, what his likes and dislikes were.

Hours later, we both woke up in the car leaning on each other. It was 8:00am and was late to drop my daughter off and obviously I was going to be late for work. There was still snow on the ground from that real bad snow we just had few weeks back, which meant that the buses were going to be off schedule. Metro never did recover from the storms on time. Plus, I still had to get dressed and get her ready. I thought that it was about to be a long week. But, as long as I saw him, it was worth it. He dropped me and the baby off then he went to work.

Hours later, my phone went off.

REXX 10:00am
Good morning Beautiful

My heart dropped and started racing. He was the sweetest guy. He showed me certain things just in that one conversation and he didn't even know it. I just really liked whatever vibe we had. I was texting him throughout the day and we agreed to meet up later that night after he got off work.

Tish hired me to work for her cleaning company Top 2 Bottom Cleaning. I did that pastime to get extra money for the baby. Tish called me out into the living room and started showing me apartments. I was looking at her with confusion. Shyt I thought we had a good thing going. She was saying that it was time for me to jump out there on my own. And honestly, I agreed. I actually did want my own space. So it was understood from that point on, I was gonna apply myself.

My phone went off.

REXX 11:00am
Hey beautiful, I want
to see you.

Me 11:15am
Hey boo I can't
my baby is sick.

REXX 11:17am
Damn boo ok ill
see you later then.

Me 11:18am
Ok boo.

Me and Masiah was chilling at my sister and her baby father house when Rexx was texting me. My baby wasn't feeling well, she had a fever and wasn't really eating or drinking. Masiah wasn't the clingy type and although she was sick she still wanted to laugh and play.

My phone went off.

REXX 12:30pm
I'm outside babe.

Me 12:31pm
Huh, I'm at my
sisters house
come there.

Now in my mind, I'm like *why the fuck would he come and I told him my baby was sick?* It's been a few weeks, so he knew certain things… but when my kid is sick, I stick around her for the most part. I was clueless and was ready to curse his ass out but I couldn't do that to him.

I walked outside the building because around Cypress Creek, the buildings were warm like in the 70's. As soon as I saw him pull up, I hopped in his car.

"Rexx, I told you-"

He put his finger on my lips and smiled. "I picked up a few things so that Si could feel better." I looked at the bag by my feet and saw a variety of baby medicine, tea, soup, and a few toys. "I know what you told me. I just wanted to see you." He flashed his smile again and I was hooked. Just like that smh.

"You cute or whateva." I kissed him and melted. "I gotta go take care of my baby. Thank you Rexx."

I looked at his beautiful face and knew that he was my soulmate. I stepped out the car and closed the door. Things were finally looking up. Maybe God really felt bad for me for once.

THE MURDER

December was surprisingly warm. The Redskins was playing at home and they were on the road to winning. The previous night, there was confusion about some money with a friend for a hotel for a birthday party. The morning of December 20, Rexx came home from work around 12:00, 12:30. I was laying across the bed when he walked his cute ass through the door. Turrell and Masiah ran to greet him at the bedroom door with hugs and kisses. Those two were so pressed for him, it was crazy. At the same time, they were still mommy's girls. He got undressed down to his shorts, a wife beater, and some socks, started rubbing my butt and started general conversation.

He kissed me on the lips as he said, "Hi baby."

"Hey babe, how was work?"

"Work was work, I'm tired a little bit though. Have you talked to Dee? I pose to be going to get that money today."

"Nah, I haven't talk to her but I doubt if she comes here after the way this situation played out. I mean, she been fucking up and she not going to want to be around knowing that it is a money issue yet again."

In my mind, I felt bad as hell because all he did was try to help. I was upset as well for him making the agreement with someone without even consulting with me. I feel like we wouldn't even be in this situation five days before Christmas and ten days before rent if he had he only opened his mouth. Making assumptions is almost never good, but it happened. Even the way I found out about the whole little arrangement blew me more so because I was the last to know. Furthermore, I would have said hell no we not helping because it's been too many money situations dealing with Dee. But in his defense, he assumed I knew about her asking him for the favor because he figured I sent her to him. Smh. I asked, "What you getting me for Christmas?"

Rexx chuckled. "Girl idk, you so damn picky now. What you getting me for Christmas?"

"Whateva you want, sir. When are you suppose to be going to get the money?"

 "Well now, but you know I ain't moving til this game goes off. Come on now, you know me better than that."

"Damn my bad I was just asking."

The Redskins were playing the Bills and the Skins were doing their thing. The only time I could get some attention from him during the game was commercial and maybe halftime. As soon as a commercial came on he started to show me these different decks of cards that he was so infatuated with. The cards were cute, but I didn't even know where the infatuation came from. Since my baby was interested, I was interested, too. That interest was cut short when there was a knock at the door.

It was Dee. She came through to apologize for the situation and she was gonna make sure Rexx gets his one hundred and forty dollars. She also told Rexx that she will ride with him over to her baby father's house to pick up the money. Rexx explained to her that he don't move when the game is on so he will go after the game. We went back upstairs to finish watching the game. I went downstairs to cook. I made smothered turkey wings, cabbage, and rice. I had to make baked chicken for Rexx because he didn't like the slimy texture of turkey wings, but he had the same sides. I ended up eating my plate during the game because I was starving. I made his plate and put it in the microwave. I also had a hair appointment for Turrell, so I was taking her hair out. I had a house full of kids. My nephew, my two kids, Dee son, and my Godson Braylyn. Towards the end of the game, I started to wash the kids up as well as finished watching the rest of the game with the hubby.

Dee told Rexx that she told her baby father that they were on the way and Rexx got up out the bed an said "I'll be back baby."

"Nah boo, wait I want to go. It's not gonna take me that long to get ready. That way we can just go straight to the appointment for Turrell's hair appointment afterwards."

"Nah babe, I'm tryna go and come right back. I'm just getting money and coming back. Warm my food up for me please, I'll see you in a sec."

After fifteen minutes went by I decided to give him a call because it felt like he been gone for too long.

Rex answered on the second ring. "Hello?"

"Boo where are you at? What's taking so long?"

"Nikki you know that the game was home today and I couldn't go around the stadium. I had to go the Brightseat Road way."

I said ok and finished washing the babies up. During one of the baths I heard Rex ringtone go off, I was late getting to the phone because I had the baby in the tub at the time, but when I got to the phone I really couldn't hear much but was sound like someone was trying to say something but I didn't think anything of it. I hung up and went back into the bathroom to wash up another kid when my phone went off again so I jogged to the phone this time, I answered the phone to hear what sounds like laughter. For some reason my heart had dropped and was beating faster than a guilty man in court waiting to be sentenced. I wasn't panicking though, I was just listening not knowing how to feel. I started to get mad because I was trying to figure out what the hell was going on.

A man then took the phone and started to tell me that a young man was shot two times in the chest. I let the phone hit the floor and I got light headed. My body began to get hot, my head starting spinning and all I could think was to rush out the house. I felt so scared I started tripping because Rexx took my car so I totally forgot that I had another vehicle outside. Then it dawned on me that my expedition was fucked up, but I was gonna for damn sure take my chance to get to him. I looked back right before I left out the door I told my oldest Masiah be a big sister and be good I'll be back.

All I was thinking was *what the fuck happened? Was is he okay?* I lost my mom a year before, I literally wasn't gonna be able to take it if something happened to the love of my life. My best friend. My partner in crime. I just really hoped and wished and prayed that he was okay.

Pulling up to the Jericho Residences, surprisingly I was able to drive up to the scene.

The sight that I was getting ready to see was not one I was prepared for. As I walked up, I looked to the left by the door. There he was, laying lifeless on the cold ground because by now it was dark. His blood was pouring out of his body, paramedics were trying to revive him or keep him alive. There was blood everywhere. I felt the life leave my body. My soul was gone and I was no stranger to how this goes. After a while, they picked him up off the ground and put him on the stretcher and his arm flew off the stretcher. I knew right then and there he was gonna die. So, at that point, I fought to get to him. It took three cops to hold me down, all I literally wanted to do was kiss him and tell him I loved him before he died. Despite my efforts, I was unsuccessful.

Rexx left out the house with grey sweat pants a white tee and the two-toned grey new balance. I tried so hard to keep the happy living memory in my head but I couldn't help but think the worst. Although he was breathing when we left the scene, I knew he wouldn't be for long. All I could do was scream and cry. I never cried this hard in my life. I didn't want to live anymore. I was done. I was at a loss.

I asked the cop could I take my car to follow the ambulance so that I wouldn't have to worry about my truck cutting off. He gave me the go ahead and I followed the ambulance. I was so lost that I ended up passing the damn ambulance.

Arriving at PG Hospital, I was almost immediately thrown in a room. In that moment, I knew what was up because I went thru this a year ago with my mom. Nothing but bad news comes after that. The surgeon walked into the room and he sat down. Just like that he said, "I'm sorry, but there was nothing else we could do. He was shot in the heart and in the lower part of the abdomen. We tried everything, but he died on the table."

Turrell was dead. My fiancé, my kids father, the love of my life was gone.

To be continued....